*Can the flame be rekindled
once it's been doused from pain?*

Drama Queens
CALL OFF YOUR DOGS

L.U. ANN

Drama Queens: Call Off Your Dogs

By L U Ann

Drama Queens: Call Off Your Dogs Copyright © 2014 by L U Ann

Disclaimer: This is the work of fiction. All characters, organizations, and events portrayed in this novel are either products of the author's imagination or are used fictitiously. Any resemblance to actual persons, living or dead, events or locales is entirely coincidental.

The author acknowledges the trademark status and trademark owners of various products referenced in this work of fiction, which have been used without permission. The publication/use of these trademarks is not authorized, associated with, or sponsored by the trademark owners.

ISBN: 10:0692322647
ISBN: 13:9780692322642

Editor: Rogena Mitchell Manuscript Services
Cover Artist and Formatter: Tara Graphic
Published by L U Ann

Dedication

I dedicate this story to life and the healing power of animals. If it weren't for my dogs, this story could never have been written.

Friends and family were here and there along the way, some spotlighting more than others, but through it all, I cherish every single one of you.

~L.U. Ann

"A dog is the only creature on earth that loves you more than he loves himself."

~ Josh Billings

"Our prime purpose in life is to help others. And if you can't help them, at least don't hurt them.

~ Dalai Lama

CONTENTS

Acknowledgements

This is not going to be your average acknowledgements. I'm giving you fair warning because I need to start off by explaining myself. Although this is my fourth novel, I still have a lot to learn. I won't be able to grow as a writer if I stop writing. Sadly, I almost put my pen down when those who I thought were picking me up were, in fact, bringing me down. The indie author world is amazing, but it has its downfalls, too. Just like everything else. I do, however, believe there is much good, encouragement, and insightfulness in this world, and that if I pick and choose wisely, I can find genuine peers in the industry. My case was the crowd I surrounded myself with. I have to thank God for helping me see what was going on and helping me pick up the pieces so that I could continue to write.

See, I'm the type of person who likes to live in a happy bubble, but the problem is, I don't protect that bubble. It easily gets knocked down. Why? Because each time I rebuild my bubble, I make the walls out of cardboard and not with the right material. My family, friends, and dogs are the strong structure I've realized that give my walls strength. There is one person I need to thank for helping me see where others were attaching themselves to my bubble to destroy it, but I doubt she'd admit to anyone how amazing she truly is. Thank you, Trenda. You are an amazing friend and confidant.

I'd like to thank my husband, who painstakingly took on the role of motherhood as well as his own role along my journey to write Drama Queens. To my daughter, who reminds me every time she wants something from me that I live in my own little book world. To my son, who has made many pickups from the bus stop because I was too involved in a scene to do it myself.

i

To my dogs and cats, who remind me in some unpleasant ways that I forgot to let them out, or as they soothed and snuggled alongside when I was crying over a scene.

I'd like to thank my 'drama queens'— Renee, April, Tbird, and Amber. You ladies rock with your feedback, phone calls, and private messages offering words of encouragement. Thank you from the bottom of my heart for helping me make Drama Queens: Call Off Your Dogs what it is now. P.S. Cujo sends a lick.

To all the kind bloggers out there who I've had the pleasure to work with over the last two years—thank you will never be enough!

My editor, Rogena, who knows the blessings a pet can give us, you have been amazing to work with. Your support and enthusiasm have been a godsend.

And last, but certainly not least, I want to thank the number of animals (two and four-legged LOL) that fill my home with love. Animals are amazing creatures. Please be kind to them. Their love is pure and unconditional.

Prologue

"Thank God, I was let out of this dirty cage today. I seriously needed a break from listening to those humans cackling about this and that. I sure will miss my tail wagging friends. This human is questionable. His bright yellow pants and pink shirt are giving me a headache. Dear God, please don't let him dress me up. Wait... Oh, no, I think I'm going to be carsick!"

~ *Cujo*

2008

"Gram, that seems a little risqué to me," Mabel says handing me the rough draft of Grams weekly column. "I wonder what the people at your church think." Mabel raises an eyebrow at Gram.

"Darling, you have to live a little. Don't limit yourself to society's rules. Lord knows those rules are violated every day. I'm only doing it underhandedly. And, for the love of God, don't bring him into this. He and I have worked out an arrangement." Gram bats her lashes. How can an old woman be conniving yet look innocent at the *same* time?

Damn she's good.

I begin to read the rough draft of this week's column post:

Sunday, July 19, 2008
Drama Queens: Call Off Your Dogs

Citizens of Eufaula, Drama Mama here, and I'm going to tell you two chewable, delicious, bone-worthy reads releasing this week.

Trenda Jacobson's Wronged is projected to jump to the top of the charts quickly. Trenda brings in Alan Bird—a quiet man who had very few friends growing up. Not because others didn't like him. No, he was a loner. This behavior kept him away from the real world. With little interaction with the outside world as an adult and an experimental scientist, he found his joy in pain. Not his pain, but others. The FBI has been hunting Alan for years—almost a decade—before they discover his underground lab. When the violent acts are uncovered, will the FBI agents be able to find Alan, and most importantly, will they be able to escape being next in line?

This next one is going to be a must-read. Deliberate Intentions by Renee Gilbert is best described as a modern day Romeo and Juliet—only worse. The two main characters, Mike and Lauren, are high school sweethearts. Mike is two years older, goes to a local community college so that he can stay close to his girlfriend. He makes sacrifice after sacrifice to stay with her. Problem is, she doesn't. Lauren is brilliantly manipulating Mike as her puppet. This story looks at the problems with young-dumb love and how two teens practically escape a bright future because they are in too much of a rush to get married.

Lauren does something very sneaky to seal the deal—something that has great consequences for both of them. Will they get the love and support from their families when everything becomes clear? This one is sure to touch readers of many generations.

Quickly, I would like to take a moment to thank my readers for their support and enjoyment of this unconventional column. This marks my fifty-second column as Drama Mama. For one year, I've created quite a stir in the reader, author, and in the publishing world—and I've enjoyed every bit of it. I appreciate all the comments and can't wait to see what we discover over the next fifty-two posts.

Okay, now that we've gotten all that out of the way. Let's get onto the good stuff. People who you interact with on a regular basis can be compared to dogs. You know you have thought about it before. It can be a co-worker, friend, or possibly, a family member. Either way, canine behavior isn't exclusive to its kind. Take for instance Chihuahuas. They are small and look so innocent, but the moment you piss them off, they are attacking the leg of your pants or hiking their leg on your furniture to show you who the real boss is.

These are the true bullies of the world. Why? Because the moment you stop cuddling with your pocket pet, they turn on you. Let's have a look at the monstrous Pit bull. Their big, muscular frame has many scared to death of them. They were born with strong jaws that match their strong bodies. But guess what? They aren't going to turn on you like those little Mexican things. No, they will lick you to death and play for hours. So, when I'm looking for someone to be in my corner, I'd rather have the one that looks vicious on the outside, but has a heart of gold as opposed to the one that looks cute and cuddly, but can turn into a biting piranha at any moment.

So there you have it. Drama Mama's paw print. Until next week, keep your eyes open for those ankle biters and thanks for reading Drama Queens: Call Off Your Dogs.

"Gram, I'm going to college so that I can, hopefully, become a great writer and editor, but I can tell you now, I won't be writing stuff like this. You must've been born with a set of balls," I manage to say in all seriousness before looking at Mabel and we fall into a fit of giggles.

"Gertie, you will find people in this industry who are precisely like the dogs I described. It's best you toughen up. You will encounter some who are nice to your face, become a best friend, but will talk about you behind your back and make you sound crazy. All the while, they are the crazy ones to start with. I'm trying to teach you how to cope with these Chihuahuas of the world. Your best bet is to find a Pit bull."

My eyebrows furrow in confusion. Are people really like that?

"Sweetheart, you're young and dumb." My eyes grow at her harshness. "Oh, please, you know it as well. You need to go out and experience the world. Just watch out for needless drama and the back-stabbing bitches of the industry. I mean, come on, really? No one does drama like me." Gram smiles before walking out of the room.

"We're related to that?" Mabel whispers, watching Grams retreating form. Slowly raising my shoulders in a shrug, we glance at one another suspiciously before returning our eyes to the doorway Gram had just walked through.

"That woman is crazy," I claim.

"No doubt," Mabel agrees.

One

Tyler

I message the throb threatening to erupt from beneath my temples, clearly a result, of the mixture of *twangy* music and abundantly loud voices competing with one another. All the while, others get their thrills out of dancing in a line making fools of themselves. Reaching for the plastic bottle, I take a sip of my water and watch the older man bustle his way behind the dilapidated counter that has served patrons for many generations. I hope their Momma and Daddy taught them the decency to tip for such services. It would be a damn shame if this guy works half as hard as he does and isn't recognized for his efforts. Glasses filled with an

1

assortment of colors clink in good wishes and money changes hands as I sit here and hope this night will be over before we know it. I'm not one to go out much. A quiet night sitting under the stars sounds more appealing than seeing my buddies get drunk here at Roots 'n Boots, a popular country bar just on the fringes of our little town.

"Dude, come on. Stop being a wuss," Greg shouts loudly so that everyone in the bar can hear him as he slaps my back.

I adjust the ball cap sitting backward on my head in an effort to release some of the pent-up annoyance for Greg at this very moment. "I'm not a wuss. I just don't feel like drinking tonight." My attention returns to the hardworking man trying to earn an honest living behind the counter.

"Pussy whipped at twenty-one. Day-um!" he says, looking smug. All the while, a girl with those fake batting eyes, hangs onto every one of his words as well as his body.

My eyes quickly cut from the bottle of water resting on the countertop to Greg. "Fuck you!" I call out and give him a one-handed shove.

The girl actually whines. Oh, dear God, she's fake.

"Pa-pa-pa-pa-pusssss-ie whipped," Greg sings unaffected by my shove and getting hoots and hollers from those around.

"I don't need that shit to make me happy, Greg. And it's called love. There's a difference." Although my profession might be genuine, he rolls his eyes.

Dammit.

Greg's never going to give up. I might as well give in and get it over with so that I can get the hell out of here. "Fine, one drink and that's it. I have shit to do tomorrow."

Slapping my back again, he raises his other hand to motion for the bartender. "Round of shots, man. The pussy-whipped one is gonna do it." I pull back and shake my head no. I don't touch hard shit. *Hell no.* I learned that a long, long time ago. That shit gets you in trouble. "Ty, if you're only having one drink, I'm going to make it worth it. Now bottoms up!"

Fuck. One drink can't hurt. *Can it?*

The bartender sets a straight line of glasses in front of us and begins to fill each one. I missed something the guys had said as I was trying to convince myself that it was okay to have one drink. Swiveling around on the bar stool, I find Mike repeating his nonsense banter. I don't care for the guy too much. Mike's an ass, and the vibe I get doesn't exactly scream upstanding American, always drinking, smoking weed and doing shit that screws with your head.

Greg feels bad when his friends go out and they don't invite Mike, so he usually drags him along. I've known Greg my entire life since he happens to be my cousin. My dad and his mom are siblings. Four years my senior, he's a bit more experienced at this whole bar scene. I really couldn't care less whether I'm here or not. The other three guys joining us aren't bad. Justin, Dan, and Al have worked for Greg's booming landscaping business from the time he started it six years ago. Since we live in small town Eufaula, everyone thought it was cute when Greg began the business. We laugh now that he's sitting financially well-off and considered an honorable businessman in the community, too.

Three days. I get my girl in three days and that's all that matters. If I continue telling myself this, it will get me through tonight.

I haven't seen her since I put her on the bus back in January, just in time for spring semester. Two more years, she'll graduate, and I'm going to ask the girl of my dreams, the one who I will never let go, to marry me. Many nights, I fall asleep dreaming about how I will propose and then she will be all mine. Because she deserves the best things and I will give it to her. Forever.

In the meantime, I have a construction business to focus on. College wasn't in the cards financially for my family. Luckily, the town of Eufaula, although small, still needs home remodeling or structures built that keep us busy. It makes the time pass by a little easier sometimes, but there is always a missing void when my Gert isn't around.

Greg's hand slaps the bar, snapping me out of my thoughts. He hands me a small glass hosting the amber liquid, a round of cheers erupts as the burn of the alcohol begins to make its way down my throat.

"See? That wasn't so bad. Let's do another," Greg yells to the five of us as he watches the bartender begin to replenish our glasses. *Shit!* This is going to be a long night.

Tossing the second glass back doesn't deliver the same burn. No, instead my head begins to feel lighter as the room grows louder. As the night goes on, I quickly lose count of how many drinks I consume.

The piercing scream has me shooting up in bed only to immediately grab my head, praying it will ease the throbbing pain. "Tyler!" *Oh, shit!* Dammit, the throb.

"Gert, stop shouting. My head hurts." I try to plead as I fall back onto the bed. *What the fuck?* As the hangover begins to vanish, I look up to see... No. Please, God, no!

"Oh, my God, I can't believe you!" she shouts as tears and mascara run down her cheeks.

Oh, shit.

OH, SHIT!

What have I done?

Gertie

Scrambling toward the stairs in a frenzied fit, I gasp, trying to catch the air that was just sucked out of my lungs. I need to get out of here. The growing knot in my throat thickens with each laden step. Fingers tremble in their search to locate the handrails as I attempt to race to the front door before the person whom I'm running from catches up. I can't breathe. The familiar squeaks of the old wood can no longer be heard from the rasping stomps of each step beneath my feet.

Tears.

Stupid tears begin to sting my eyes.

Damn things cloud my vision and the door feels as if it's light years away.

My world just collided with tragedy. A heartbreaking collision, leaving me barely holding onto life support from the mess I walked in on upstairs. The reality of what I had when I woke up this morning is no longer true, and it hits hard. What I just witnessed shattered my hopes and dreams. If only I could rewind time. I know I would. I can't believe this and I can't get out of this once-cherished house fast enough.

My hand reaches to clench my chest while the other twists the knob, pulling open the door that was protecting me from intruders. The slam against the wall echoes throughout the house vocalizing my broken heart.

One step.

This is precisely why I need to focus on college and not stupid love. Whoever said love lasts forever was a moron.

Love.

Another step.

I hate that word.

One more word I detest?

Tyler.

Tyler Jackson to be exact.

Step.

Tyler is a butt-head. A big fat, stupid, *lying* ass-hat.

Ugh, I wish I felt better venting like a child. Nothing would make me happier than to stomp around and show Tyler exactly what I think of him. But, no, I can't... his ass is still in bed with bimbo. At least I *hope* he is.

He told me to go and follow my dream and that we'd be fine. Why did he... I can't deal with this. *I just don't want to.*

Did it have to be *her*? Of all people, the town tramp! Who, oh God, *has* a better body than me. Why couldn't I have captured the beautiful genes like my skinny-ass sister?

This isn't fair.

She got a better name and body, while I got stuck with... *me.*

"Grrrr..." I jump at the snarling white thing with some serious leakage dripping from its mouth. *Oh, no, he's going to eat me.* "Grrr..." It continues to growl and the fact that this thing might want to take a chomp out of my meaty flesh hits me. Not taking heed to what Gram's taught me, I turn to run away—only to miss my footing. *Ouch!*

"Cujo, behave!" a sweet voice demands while the dog's ears pull back, and it gives me a whiny groan before lying down. "Aw darling, I'm so sorry. Are you okay?" Those beautiful vocal chords chime for me while I lay sprawled out on butt-head's front lawn with my cosmetics and—*oh no, not those*—fly out of my bag, littering the meticulously kept lawn. Nervously, I advert my eyes toward the dog, tail wagging, panting, and wearing a smile as its eyes squint from the bright sun. Yeah, vicious thing is just a lump of love, all bark, and no bite. Why couldn't the dog have attacked me so that I'd be knocked out saving myself from the embarrassment and pain my heart is experiencing.

Voices yelling pull my attention toward the door I had just run out of moments before.

Shit, I need to escape. God help me if Bimbo and Butt-head see me beached on his lawn with a mess running down my cheeks and feminine condiments tossed about.

The guy with the dog, whose voice makes my body hum, stands over me concealed by the sun's rays. My eyes burn from the blinding light. I roll myself over and scramble to collect the disaster that is all over the familiar lawn.

"Gert!" Butt-head shouts pushing himself off his front porch that adorns a swing like they have on old country houses. So many nights ass-hat and I could be found on that swing listening to the quiet sounds of Eufaula, Oklahoma. Once we both started high school, the swing began learning the sounds of nature weren't all we were interested in. Friends for most of our lives, Tyler and I simply moved into boyfriend/girlfriend mode. I don't think we ever anticipated it.

One summer afternoon, we were sharing a hot fudge sundae at the local creamery. As we fought over the last bite that always held the most fudge, I won by shoving the spoon into my mouth. Only, some of the fudge landed just under my bottom lip as I sped to win the last bite. Tyler's eyes immediately darkened scaring me for a moment. Apprehensively, I wondered why his expression altered. Was he *mad*? It wasn't until his thumb reached up to run along my bottom lip, immediately drawing his thumb into his mouth, did my body react in a way it never had before. His eyes caught sight of my quickened breath. Later that night when he walked me home, his lips touched mine for the first time, and I was swept away into a fairy tale.

Only, I forgot every fairy tale has a villain, only I had mistook the villain for Prince Charming. Never has a fairy tale revealed its Prince Charming at the beginning of the story.

And my story is just beginning.

I think or I imagine.

"Gert, please." Ass-wipe stands within arm's reach now. I want to beat the ever-loving shit out of him for this.

"Please? You are saying please to me?" My eyes narrow and burn into his deep blues, the eyes I used to spend endless hours devouring. "You no longer get that privilege. I come home early for spring break to surprise you, and I find you shacking up with this tramp."

"I'm not a tramp!" Bimbo retorts with a hand on her hip while sticking out her boobs.

"Fine." I glance down at the dog making sure he doesn't want to lick my hind quarters before allowing my eyes to roam up her figure. "If you aren't a tramp, then you're a bitch, Cindy. Oh, and when did you get those?" I point to her boobs. Yeah, those have gotten bigger. Fake bimbo.

The bitch actually gasps.

Rolling my eyes, I concede. "Tyler, we're over. You threw a lifetime away for this." My arms move up and down as my eyes fixate on the town tramp in front of us. Turning back to Tyler, "You said we were *forever*." Tears spill freely.

"Gert, *please*. I'm so sorry. I got drunk last night and don't remember. Please come inside and talk. We can—" My hand flies up to stop his stupid words as I nearly smacked him in the face. I don't want to hear anymore.

Bimbo starts griping. "You don't remember, Tyler?" Her hands fly up as she turns around and storms into the house.

I'm confused, tired and heartbroken. It was a long bus ride… a nine-and-a-half hour needless bus ride, and now all I want is Gram. I need Gram. She always makes things better.

"Let me get this straight. You want me to go inside your parents' house where you were just doing God knows what? Oh, wait. I had the unfortunate reality of witnessing what you *were* doing!" I shout, throwing my arms about like a petulant child. The sun glares rays upon us as if it is a spotlight on a stage. Taking a breath, "Tyler, you aren't really sorry for breaking my heart and the future we had planned." Throwing my hands in the air, I continue. "You're sorry you got caught."

I look down at the heap of drool. "Come on, Cujo, I need a lift." All the warnings Gram instilled in me about taking a ride from strangers exit my consciousness. I will do anything to get away from Tyler and the heartache he has caused. Fucking nine-and-a-half hour bus ride and short walk from the bus stop have left me stranded.

"Of course, right this way, baby girl." My body hums to his voice. *What the hell?* And why is this guy in small town America? I've never seen him or the slobbering mess before. I haven't been gone for that long. *Have I?*

Remembering why my heart is breaking, I look up at butt-head, who was not only my best friend, but my boyfriend when I woke up this morning. "Goodbye, Tyler." With teeth clenched, I turn on my heels following the obnoxiously loud pants from the wagging four-legged cootie and flea-ridden critter.

"No, Gert! No. Please don't leave me." As I flip my hair over my shoulder, I catch his fallen form in my peripheral vision on the lawn where I had just left.

It takes everything I have to continue putting one step in front of the other rather than run to Tyler. My heart is bathed in grass stains as if it's the knees of our old jeans from the lawn. I had always felt this was my second home ever since I could remember. Sensing the control over my crumbling heart vanishing, I know I need to get out of here.

"Baby girl, come on and get in." If I weren't so hurt, I would take time to digest the hot pants standing before me along with his sleek black mustang, but Cujo's presence brings me back to reality. He jumps into the front seat. Am I supposed to share a seat with that thing?

Can my day get any worse?

Damn dog.

Two

*"Why are humans constantly hissing at each other like those
obnoxious cats I try to stay clear of? If only they looked at how a
pack of dogs treats each other, I could live in a much more
peaceful world."*

~ *Cujo*

Three years later...

Gertie

The pounding rumbles through my head and disrupts my
pleasant dream where Adam Levine chose me to be his
wife in some weird—no, definitely not weird... It was a
heavenly, blissful bachelor show. I crack my eyes open to
find the sun peeking through the blinds causing me to curse
Mother Nature that it's still not the middle of the night. I'm
not a morning person and never once claimed to be. Chris
Brown's song, *Don't Wake Me Up*, is extremely poignant
at this moment.

I throw the covers over my head, hoping to drown out the noise. I don't want to get up yet. My Egyptian and Pima Cotton sheets are one of the few things I had splurged on. My salary might be healthy, but I've never been one to spend needlessly. My roommate, on the other hand, is a different story.

Oh, holy shit.

I grab my pillow and bury my head securing my hands on top to hold it tight over my ears. Who the hell could be showing up at my door at this hour? *Complete and utter rudeness!*

"Go away!" I yell. *Seriously?* This is Sunday morning.

Two days.

I only get two days all to myself to sleep in and some jerk is taking one of those days from me. Not just that, this might be my last full weekend to sleep late. The pounding continues, but a little more pressing as I lay here staring at the ceiling. They don't seem to be going away anytime soon and sleep appears to be pointless and out of the question. Thank you, asshole. Throwing my leg in the air, I kick off my precious covers and slowly roll off the bed. I untwist my t-shirt and shorts before wiping the junk that had built in my eyes as I slept. It's most likely from crying happy tears thanks to the one and only swoon-worthy rock star, who had chosen me to be his wife. Ugh! Why did I have to wake up? He chose me, *dammit.*

Heaving a sigh, I slip my toes into my favorite flip-flop slippers, sway toward the front door wishing I could first make a quick stop in the kitchen for my morning fix.

Instead, whoever is on the other side of the door will see reality rear its ugly head. As much as I want to lick my future husband's delectable abs, I need to get rid of the termite who stole my dream. Still half asleep, I open the door and my heart stops.

Literally.

Dead stop.

I stare blinking. It has to be a mirage. The heavens wouldn't be that cruel. *Would they?*

"Gert," he whispers softly, barely registering the words. When I don't respond, he questions again. "Gert?" His forehead wrinkles, and a frown replaces his stoic features from just a moment ago.

Nothing. I have nothing that wants to come out. The saying cats got your tongue may or may not apply here.

"Gert!" He moves toward me placing a hand on each shoulder giving me a nudge. "Blink, baby. I have wanted… for so long…"

What?

His pause allows me to cut in. "Baby?" I say as tears begin to seep from my eyes. I shake my head and step away as I remove his hands. "You don't get to call me that," I say straining to find my voice. His face falls and morphs into shock as I continue, "What are you doing here?"

"Please give me a chan—"

"A chance? What chance do you want me to give you? A chance to explain what happened that night or a chance to explain why you never..." I push on his chest causing him to stagger backward, "...never fought for me. For us?"

His face screams exhaustion, but I don't care. Not after throwing our future away like he had.

I grab my head and spin away trying to gather the storm of thoughts running so fast and hard screaming through my mind. Squeezing my eyes, I turn around and say, "You don't belong here. I want you to leave."

I don't bother waiting for him to walk out.

He had better.

My focus turns to something simple. Coffee. At least it doesn't take a lot of brain cells to make it.

Sensing a presence behind me, I haul off and slap the victim also known as Tyler Jackson. "I said leave." My hands push him back hoping he gets the picture.

"Gert, please. I need to explain." He exhales.

Clenching my fists and throwing them down to my sides, I scream, "Your actions over the last few years have explained enough. NOW... LEAVE!" I scream before running back to my room praying this day can have a restart. Fuck the coffee. Tears run rampantly. Why is he here? Why now? It has been three years and he now shows his face? Has he lived with the constant reminder of what we could have had? My stomach wants to lurch from my heart breaking all over again. Memories flood my mind, and I can't help but question why he did what he did all those years ago.

The wonderful aroma of coffee wakes me hours later after crying myself to sleep. I take a long deep breath to inhale the wonderful smell. I search through swollen eyes for my slippers and then to follow the scented trail. Opening the door, I wrap my arms around my waist to keep the blizzard of pain that is flowing through my veins at bay and proceed toward the kitchen.

I find Mabel on her laptop sitting at the kitchen island sipping a cup of heavenly joe. Rubbing my eyes to conceal their sadness, I grab a cup keeping my back to Mabel for as long as I possibly can without raising suspicion. I know she'll find out soon enough if she doesn't already know. How did she not wake up to the commotion? Dismissing the thought, I just want these next few minutes to be inside my head without others polluting it with their two-cents.

Lucky for me, she's enthralled in whatever she's reading. Most likely, it's our favorite column. Since we no longer live in Eufaula, getting our local hometown newspaper delivered isn't possible. Thank heavens for the internet. While the Keurig does it's magic of warming up, I take a deep breath before finding the setting for the largest cup.

"Good morning, Gertie..." Mabel interrupts my internal thoughts leaving her acknowledgment open-ended as if she wants to say more. Or maybe I just need to wake up and stop reading shit into shit.

"Morning," I grumble as I add the unhealthy stuff that makes my coffee taste the way I've grown accustomed to drinking it.

"Have you seen today's column?" she questions as I grab my mug and take a sip settling on a stool next to her. The first sip is always the best. I mean, if they can bottle that first sip and sell it, someone would be a billionaire.

"No, can I see?" I ask motioning toward her screen.

"Sure." She takes a moment to study me. "But only if you promise to share whatever this is." Mabel twirls her index finger around in a circular motion as if I'm in need of dissection.

I roll my eyes and scoff. "Just give it to me." She slides her laptop over and it doesn't take long to see there have already been a number of social media likes and comments.

"Sounds like someone needs to talk to their sister about something." Mabel raises an eyebrow at my barely-alive form. "You look like death."

Ignoring my sister's rudeness, I ask, "What did she do this week?

Mabel laughs while I begin to read our Grams column. Every Sunday, she publishes controversial topics in the Daily Indian Journal. Not only Eufaula's, but Oklahoma's oldest running newspaper. Gram's been working there since they opened in 1908. Okay, okay, I exaggerated. I know she's only sixty-eight, but, man, does it seem like she was around when God created the Heavens and Earth. I think it was Gram who said, 'Let there be light' because the woman brings it everywhere she goes. She could also be a serpent and could get anyone to do what she wants besides eating fruit from a tree. The woman is very persuasive and couldn't care less what others think. It's one of the things I admire about her.

Sunday, March 2, 2014
Drama Queens: Call Off Your Dogs

Citizens of Eufaula, Drama Mama here, and I'm gonna tell you about two tail waggin' lickable reads releasing this week.

If you want a sit on the edge of your seat, suspenseful read, look no further than Spike by Alisha Regan. Spike comes with baggage. A troubled childhood moving from one foster family to another, he finally finds his true home and family in one of the worst gangs known to Seattle's Police Department. The police refer to him as a ghost because every lead comes up empty. At every turn, he's disappeared, but they know where he's been. He leaves his mark that law enforcement have become too familiar with. When he catches sight of Donna, will he be able to be able to hide from his demons? Will the ghost finally be revealed?

The highly anticipated Iron Cloud by NY Times bestselling author Eleanor Buck releases Tuesday and is already causing an uproar in the author world that this is going to be better than any of her previously published works. I can't wait to sink my teeth into this. Iron Cloud is a local hole in the wall diner tucked away on a small abandoned airport runway. A runway that used to be alive and thriving with tires as they descended the heavens or left it to reach new heights. Jennifer is a waitress at the Iron Cloud where she meets Dan, who features a striking resemblance to herself. After being kidnapped at a young age, she didn't know her family. Her family and friends thought she was dead. Two years ago, she escaped torture by the skin of her teeth and ran. Finding this hole in the wall diner to make a few dollars so she could move on to a more permanent situation she finally felt safe. Only, when she looked at the guy standing before her, she wasn't sure how safe she truly was. Eleanor is bound to electrify readers as this one woman embarks finding who she really is.

Okay, now onto the good stuff. You know I'll never leave a hydrant untouched. It's my job to enlighten you on the poop dropping around the author world. So, here it goes.

If you've been living under a rock, you may not know that most authors form relationships with bloggers. These are people like you and me who love to read and write how they feel about what they read. Most give their honest opinion aiding the public with choosing some amazing books. Then there are those who have their tongues on their rears and rate books four and five stars when they are honestly a one or two. The current market is overwhelmingly saturated with authors willing to write just about anything. 'Look, Uncle Johnny got a new mole on his rear. Rhonda's making out with the mailman and her husband knows. Or they've been around each other since their mums gave birth, so it's only expected that Steph and Dick be arranged to marry at their ripe age of eighteen.' Who the hell cares? Am I right? Anyone can write something like that, but a good, meaty book needs substance and a story, pups! What happened to writers taking their time to write quality instead of pushing their bowels to defecate all over the market?

So, it's only natural that readers are being exposed to crap and think it's beautiful. Today, these readers are becoming authors. Wake up people! You may have a story to tell, but it doesn't mean you can write a complete book that is worth my time and most of America's time, too. Maybe spend some time volunteering at your local animal shelter bathing dogs, scooping poop, or expelling anal glands, because you're more likely to gain success doing that than writing waste.

There you have it, ladies and gentlemen. Drama Mama's opinion. Until next week, thanks for reading Drama Queens: Call Off Your Dogs.

My heavy heart from this morning's encounter lightens a little and I manage a giggle. I shake my head at the crazy woman who tried to raise me to be this strong, independent woman. I'm not sure I'll ever measure up. I wonder first how she has the gall to write stuff like that and publish the material, and also, if I am, or ever will be, the person she pushed me to be. I clear my throat to hide my emotions before saying, "Does she care that she pisses half of the author world off when she says shit like that?"

"I knew I should have changed my last name," Mabel quips throwing her head down onto her folded arms.

I shrug. I've often wondered that many times myself. Gram has been mentioned many times in the published world for her unfiltered words. By some big names, too.

She doesn't hold back. No, she tells it like she sees it. One of the things I admire about her—most of the time.

Gram has a peculiar—

"Hey, remember to tell her we went to church this morning," Mabel moans beneath her arms. While I stare at the computer for a moment, Mabel turns her head to the side, and asks, "So why was Tyler here?"

Nearly choking on a sip of coffee I had just taken, I cough until air finds its way back into my lungs. "How did you know? Were you awake? I mean... yeah... I was loud enough... I think. I don't know... how he—"

"Whoa! Slow down," Mabel says sitting up. "Stop babbling. Dear Lord, you're giving me a headache." I stare and wait for her to answer my question, but the phone rings. Springing from her stool, she exclaims, "I'll get it." *Nice save, Mabel.*

"Hello... Oh, good morning, Grams. How are you? ... Good... I know... Uh huh... No, it's okay..." What the hell are they talking about?

I hold out my hand, "Can I talk to Gram, please?" Mabel's doubtful eyes confirmed when she shook her head no. I give her the finger and walk to my room to enjoy the rest of my coffee. Mabel whispers something, and I turn around to her locked stare. She gives me a tight-lipped smile. It's too early to examine what the two are talking about. Well, maybe not too early since it's close to noon now, but I have a sinking suspicion what the two ladies are cackling about anyway, and I have no interest in putting more thought into him.

Placing my coffee on the nightstand, I jump back in bed with my laptop.

Hours later, I'm sitting around a heap of papers, laptop screaming for a break, and my glasses sitting snug on my nose. I finally feel confident about meeting my new boss tomorrow. All of the stories are edited and ready for submission. Shutting the screen, I fall back onto my pillows. I close my eyes, but the only thing I see is Tyler. Why did he have to do this now?

My stomach grumbles, and from the time on my watch, it's close to dinner. Quickly compiling the mess into something a little more orderly, I jump up and find Mabel in the living room.

"And what are your plans tonight?" she asks.

"I don't have any other than relaxing before tomorrow." Opening the fridge, I search for something appealing.

"Your ass is so boring."

Turning around to face Mabel, I ask, "Tell me, why do we have to keep up the charade that we attend church every Sunday? We're adults."

"Um… because Gram would show up on our doorstep in her Sunday best. You know, those polyester pants that rest under her boobs that makes people think she doesn't wear a bra, along with her bright red lipstick and blue eye shadow? Do you want that to happen? Because I'm almost certain that she'll oblige," she barks, causing me to slam the cabinet door just above me. She then shrieks, "We need to get ready. The girls want us to meet them at Chaps."

"Uh, no, thank you. I'm meeting my new boss tomorrow and have no interest in getting caught up in your 'We're going out' for you to only keep me up until God knows what time. So, you girls have fun with that."

Looking over her shoulder, she eyes me hard. "Don't be such a Debi Downer. You're such a wuss. What are you afraid of..." she hesitantly continues turning the rest of the way around, "actually meeting someone?" I shake my head and allow my body to seep onto the stool. She knows better than to talk like that. What the hell kind of game is she playing?

Mabel retreats into her room and I head for the shower. My stomach no longer has any interest in food.

Why does she have to say stuff about me finding a man? I have no time for relationships. Instead of hanging out, I can go over my calendar and files. Everything needs to be in line for tomorrow. Relationships are trouble and with meeting the new editor-in-chief tomorrow, I need to have my head in the game. Word on the street is that she's a bitch and keeping my job is something important to me. Plus, I've already tried my hand at relationships, and it's not for me. Turning the water on, I begin undressing when my phone signals a text message. Worried that it could be Gram, I quickly check.

Rick: Hey, gorgeous! I'm coming to town next week. Be ready.

Me: I'm never ready four your visits.

Rick: Forget you. I want to hang with Mab.

Me: You're so mean.

Rick: Aw, you know I love you even though you're boring.

Why does everyone think I'm boring?

Me: Go away.

Rick: Cujo sends a lick. ;)

Oh dear Lord, Rick. He's been a staple in my life and the closest thing to a best friend since he gave me that ride years ago. His last message causes me to shiver, so I turn off my phone. He loves that dog more than anything in this world. He's a sweetheart, but a messy, slobbery one. I wonder if Rick and Tyler run into each other on occasion. I mean, they both live in small town America. Does Rick talk to him?

Ugh, why do I even care. Of course, I know why. Showering quickly, I return to my room.

Damn Tyler for showing his face! And why did I have to wake up this morning? I'd be Mrs. Gertrude Levine right now. Of course, I'd have to explain myself when I reached his security. He may not know it yet, but we're perfect for each other. I have no doubt whatsoever.

I plop myself onto the bed and shut my eyes for a second. At least my dreamy Adam is faithful.

"Gert." Thump, thump.

"Gert." Thump, thump.

"Gert, open this door!" Bang, bang.

I quickly open the door and run my hand through my hair to tame it. "What on earth is so urgent?" I ask as Mabel stands annoyed with her finger pointing to her watch.

"Come on, Gertie. We have twenty minutes before everyone is meeting us." Mabel sings slowly as she turns and shuts my door with her voice fading as she walks further away. I adore my sister and everything she's done for me growing up. Thinking back to what we've been through makes it difficult to ever say no.

Jiminy Crickets! I've conceded. I'm going. Arguing will get me nowhere. Although a drink or two might help calm my bouncing nerves from not only Tyler's unexpected appearance, but also, the anticipation of meeting my new boss tomorrow.

Wait.

"Who all is going to be there?" I yell back.

Silence…

Heels pounding the pavement, "Mabel, slow down. My feet hurt." What was I thinking grabbing these shoes as Mabel nearly drug me out of the apartment? Just once, I'd like to be able to say no to her. The couple of blocks to Chaps seem so much further in these shoes.

"Stop whining. We're almost there." She struts ahead in her skinny ass jeans, fuck-me heeled boots, and with her beautiful blonde hair blowing in the wind like one of those music videos. *Oh, Adam.* Perchance, the one and only Adam and I can pick up where we left off this evening. I only pray he chooses me again. As I chuckle to myself, Mabel stops walking to give me a pointed stare disrupting the stream of foot traffic around us. *Whatever.* I intended the chuckle to be silent.

Averting her attention, I said, "I know we will be there soon. The trouble is you're walking too fast. What's your rush anyway? They're going to be there regardless of when we arrive. Ten or thirty minutes doesn't faze those girls. They are most likely causing a commotion on the dance floor by now anyway. So, can you slow it down a bit for me to catch my breath?" I pant not worrying who bears witness to our conversation.

"Just one more block. You can make it." I roll my eyes and slow down. Mabel can speed walk her fit body to Chaps if she wants. These legs don't want to be sore tomorrow so she can continue tearing up the sidewalk while I just stroll.

Three

"My human was gone for three hours, what was I supposed to do ... play with myself? Okay, so maybe it was more like five minutes. Humans need to remember us dogs don't have a sense of time. I got bored and decided to find out if human was hiding one of my toys in the sofa cushion. How am I the bad guy here? I needed something to do. Regardless. Do. Not. Leave. Me!"

~ *Cujo*

Tyler

What a messed up week. One problem after another. On top of everything weighing on my shoulders at home, I don't even know how I still have a construction company after the numerous inspection failures we received at multiple locations. I think the inspectors' office needs to find something better to do than nit-pick shit that's not fucking structural. It's safe. Isn't that what ultimately matters? No, inspectors just look for stupid shit like one of the guys forgetting to put his ladder away or, at another site, the damn permit blew off in a storm and no one realized it was gone. Now, I understand the safety issue with the ladder, but it's out in the middle of nowhere and no one lives there. There's caution signs posted everywhere along with posts that say keep the fuck out. Well, okay, fine. I might go spray paint the word 'fuck' just for the hell of it after this shit.

Greg: Dude, you there?

Me: Yeah. Everything okay?

Greg: Your mom just wanted to know.

Me: I'm here. Staring at the doors.

Greg: Get some liquid courage. You might need it.

Me: Fuck you and beer in hand now.

Greg: No, thanks. I like women.

Rolling my eyes, I decide it's best to ignore Greg.

Taking a swig of my beer, the thoughts that have haunted me all day return. Gertie turned white as a ghost when our eyes met once she finally answered the door. She's beautiful, even with her hair looking like a bird's nest. I don't know what the hell kind of reaction I was expecting showing up on her doorstep this morning, but the one I got nearly gutted me. I hate that it's taken so long for me to get—

My phone vibrates distracting me.

Rick: Yo Dickwad. Where are you?

Me: I'm here.

For the Love of God, these people need to leave me alone. My nerves are shot as it is. I don't need anyone else breathing down my back.

Rick: You had better smack some of that ass!

Me: I'm powering off my phone.

I do just that and put it back in the side holster before Greg, Rick, or God knows who messages me again. I need to remain concentrated on those doors.

While I wait, I thank God my construction company is still running because my father would be rolling around in his grave if I lost his baby. His business was very important to him. It wasn't profitable as it is now while growing up, but he was proud of it. I can't say I blame him. I'm pretty damn proud of what I've done with it over the last couple of years.

He was hesitant when I tried to sell him on the idea of expanding our construction to docks, but when I took him on a boat ride around Eufaula Lake, he understood. After all, building a dock is much like building a deck. Only in water.

We expanded our services and the company tripled in size. Eufaula Lake is a huge reservoir with six-hundred miles of shoreline. More and more homes nowadays want to take advantage of lake living and what it has to offer. And Dad, thankfully, took a chance on my idea and was able to see it blossom.

To have buried Dad two weeks ago was incredibly hard. I not only lost my dad, but he wanted nothing more than to see Gertie before he passed away. Sadly, Dad's health deteriorated quickly, and I wasn't able to reach out to Gertie in time. I couldn't leave his side. With the push from an old lady with a laundry list of ulterior motives, I am here now.

I remember the day Gram barged into my family's home telling me exactly what she thought of me. *A pile of poo* were her exact words among many more. She refused to see me for the longest time. However, one day she showed up on my doorstep and within minutes, she was embracing me and also embraced someone else who owns half of my heart. She told me I needed to spend a year in *her* purgatory for the horrible sin I committed that caused her granddaughters' pain. She said after a year, she felt I had suffered enough.

At first, I tried my hardest to get Gertie back. No one would tell me where she was. I made so many trips to her campus trying to find her. To explain. But, honestly, there wasn't anything to explain. I fucked up—*royally*. It was groveling that was needed. I wasn't beyond getting on my hands and knees begging to move heaven and earth for her to take me back. Within days, Mabel had changed all her numbers and of course, Gertie disappeared off the face of the earth after finding me in bed with Bimbo. To this day, Gertie owns the other half of me, I'll never get it back. It's hers and rightfully so.

Waking up the next morning, and not having any recollection of what had happened, was the worse feeling in the world. Wait, let me take that back. Gertie walking in and finding me with someone else in bed was the worse feeling in the world. I hate myself for betraying her with the town tramp.

I'm sorry. I shouldn't speak ill of Cindy, who everyone refers to as Bimbo or the town tramp, like that. I didn't have to sleep with her, but I did. As Dad would say, 'When you go, boy, you go big.' Shaking my head, I try to rid the painful look on Gertie's face from my memory. My attention returns to the doors when an old friend finally walks through and my face lights up. It's only a matter of time now before the one I'm waiting for walks in.

"You made it!" she cries looking so woman-like, but dare I say anything about how pretty she is? She's more of a sister to me.

"Of course," I say pulling her into a hug.

"How is she?" Mabel questions.

"Good. Doing really good."

"Awesome. I need to make a trip home to see her. If only Gertie will get over herself and go home…" Mabel sheepishly turns her head away.

"It's okay. So… where is she?"

Pulling back, she slaps my arm and rolls her eyes. "You know where she is. She's a slowpoke and likes to take her sweet ass time. I finally sped ahead excited to see you." Mabel crosses her arms and rubs them to warm up before looking around for her friends. She spots them quickly and waves them over to join us.

I smile, hoping someone else is as excited to see me as Mabel is. She spends a minute introducing me to her friends, and I wait patiently while sneaking glances at the door. Mabel eyes me suspiciously. I shake my head at her pushiness. I already explained the purpose of my visit, and she should be elated I'm finally here. I've rehearsed what I want to tell Gertie so many times I can probably recite it forward and backward.

Now, I just have to remind myself not to screw this up.

Four

*"What was I thinking getting up from my nice cozy spot? Oh,
that's right. Damn squirrel thought he could enter Gram's yard.
How dare that rodent think this is his territory. More
importantly, why does it not bother my human, Mr. Prissy Pants,
that the varmint is trespassing? I'm watching it run straight up a
tree whacking its tail up and down. How rude! And Mr. Prissy
Pants is yelling at me for speaking my mind? I always get
blamed."*

~ Cujo

Gertie

Quickly, Mabel disappears and I find myself caught up in
the pretty surroundings. March nights can be cold in
Houston. Today it hit the high twenties and if I weren't
stressed about tomorrow or irritated about tonight, I would
have paid a little more attention and dressed appropriately.
The clean sidewalks and picturesque street reminds me of
our tiny one-road downtown back home. Large trees create
canopies over the short storied businesses with windows lit
giving a false sense of security, but one that's warming.

Winter weathered plants recently replaced by spring flowers adorn benches as they line storefronts offering a spot to rest, most likely from sisters like mine. I hope this cold spell doesn't kill them. Spring is my favorite season. Memories of past springs have me missing Eufaula. Well, except for the storms that bring the threat of tornados. Those always scared the crap out of me. The quiet nights and open morning sky. You could see for miles and miles. Afternoons spent with my feet splashing in the lake behind Grams home with...

Ugh!

I used to enjoy a slower paced lifestyle. Here you see cluttered buildings and everyone's in a rush. Although, unlike here, the small community of Eufaula is full of gossip and everyone knows everyone else's business. I wish I could go back, but there isn't anything promising for me there. At least here, I can fade into the crowd. I mean, how can I go back? I'm sure everyone knows what happened. Not only that, but also everything, I mean everything... will remind me of Tyler. We were inseparable all our lives. I just wish he hadn't shown up. Immersing myself in college and then my job at Simple Luxury is what has found me much success.

The *one* thing that hurts the most is leaving Gram. She's more woman than I'll ever be capable of becoming. With her numerous church activities and her job at the newspaper, she stays plenty busy.

Passing an elderly lady with a lap dog sitting by her feet, I smile. "Ma'am, may I?" I ask making sure it's okay to pet her dog.

"No, sweetheart. He doesn't like strangers."

"Oh, um... okay." I look between her and the dog trying to calculate how much damage a cute little thing can cause when it's lip rises and sets as if he is about to snap. I jump back. "Thanks for the heads up," I reply to the sweet old lady while the dog continues to snarl. "Have a good evening." I end our conversation and continue to Chaps. I'm sure Mabel is irritated I wasn't following her like a little puppy.

Picking up my pace, I look down to make certain I don't stumble over my own feet. I know it's only a couple more storefronts before I'm at the familiar pub where I've spent one too many nights helping Mabel's drunk ass home. The familiar crack in the sidewalk tells me I'm here. Taking a deep breath, I gather the strength to defend myself off drinking anything Mabel gives me. She has a tendency to order drinks that are above my ability to handle. I'll just have a couple of beers. My thought is the liquid courage is necessary for helping me get my mind off the drama of Tyler and my interview tomorrow.

Lost in my thoughts, I blindly walk into the crowded bar barely hearing the bouncer greet me by my first name. Turning back, I wave at Sam. He's such a sweet guy and has a beautiful family I've had the privilege of meeting a few times.

Bam!

"Shit, I'm sor—" My insides battle while my eyes bug out of their sockets. Iridescent blues that take me far away to somewhere in the Caribbean meet mine and a smile plays on his lips. "Sorry," I say to the stranger while I drool all over myself. Stupid me. I need to get a beer now!

Pushing my way through bodies, I reach the bar and try to gather my thoughts after ordering my courage. After taking a sip, the song battle known as *Walk This Way* by Aerosmith and Run DMC streams through the speakers having me look for Mabel. When I find her, she's wearing a huge smile. This is our song. "Excuse me," I tell the mob of bodies as I rush to my sister. This has been a song we've been singing since we were little girls dancing around Grams living room making fools of ourselves, but having a blast at the same time.

Mabel with a beer in her hand as well closes her eyes as the lights bounce to the beat. I move in close. Aerosmith begins and Mabel, using her beer bottle as a microphone, sings along with the '1, 2, 3, 4.' Quickly, I interrupt mimicking Run DMC with my makeshift microphone to their hip-hop lyrics while pushing Mabel back where she stands patiently waiting for her turn. That turn being when she tells me to 'walk this way.' We continue our lyrical battle, and when it's over, I'm ready for another beer. Turning around, I come to a stop with one firm chest. *Holy hotness!* My eyes travel up finding the guy I ran into earlier who was smirking at us.

Another song plays while I stand wondering if I should leave the dance floor. His free hand reaches out to my waist pulling me into his body where I immediately ignite into flames. Looking down into my eyes, he moves his hips ever so slightly inviting me to follow his lead. *Only it feels nothing like when Tyler and I used to dance together.*

Thoughts of my one love send a shiver through my bloodstream. Thinking about dancing with him is *utter* bullshit. I need to close my eyes and enjoy now. The seductive melody has the guy's grip tightening. Did he mean to do that? I can't let this happen. He's not Tyler— *Oh!* His hips move even more causing an ache to build.

His head slowly moves down, our eyes lock until they're out of view where his warm breath tickles my ear. "Damn, Freckles, you have a gorgeous body." *Swoon, sigh, and shiver. Fuck, fuck, fuck!*

Freckles?

Closing my eyes, I will the storm to still as it builds in my lower region. It's been awhile.

A long while.

Something like three years.

Shit, I need to stop, but *damn,* it feels too good... I refuse to do relationships. My work is so much more important. More predictable.

Work! That's it. Focus, Gertie. Stay focused.

"I'm sorry," I scream over the music. His eyes don't give away any disappointment. He's stoic. "I didn't mean to give you the wrong impression..." I slowly back away in pursuit to find Mabel, but my eyes can't leave his. I'm hypnotized.

Finally, he steps closer and reaches for my waist again, pulling my clumsy body into his, and leans forward to speak. "Relax, Freckles, and feel it." And with that, I'm a heaping pile of mush.

Hips collide erupting a pulsating ache that could be from the bass streaming through the speaker or possibly deeper within. My eyes close. It's all too much. Fingers brush along the side of my face before they grasp my hair pulling my head back. His tongue licks my neck from the base to my chin and our eyes lock. Dark and intoxicating eyes glare back. He spins me around to break the spell as he places his lips—fine ass lips, on my ear. "Feel that, Freckles?" His hand slides to my lower abdomen pulling me closer. "That, Freckles, is me wanting you." *Shit, fuckity, fuck, fuck.* His heated breath sends shivers down my spine. Why do I like him calling me a pet name? Movements like this should be outlawed in all fifty states. I'm swept away for a moment.

He nips and sucks my earlobe, intensifying the overstimulated nerves within, and I lean my head to the side giving him more access. My eyes open for a moment and my body turns cold.

Tyler.

Suddenly, I can't breathe. The air is gone. The earth stops its rotation. I stare into the eyes of the only lifelong best friend I've ever had. What the fuck is he doing here? Confused, I glance around and find Mabel's shocking stare. Why is she shocked? *Seriously?*

Did she invite him here? If so, how could she do this to me? Doesn't she realize the heartache he's put me through? What he did was unforgivable. I look back at Tyler and wish I hadn't. His eyes sparkle with sadness and perhaps a tear. How dare him show up now and… Wow, I must have been half-asleep to not recognize that his body has changed. I gulp and almost swallow my tongue.

Shit! No, Gert, he's bad. *Bad, bad, bad, bad, bad!* Am I not allowed to move on? It's been three years. He's never been here, he's never fought for me. No, he quit. Well, fuck him.

Turning around, I grab the guy's hand and head for the exit. Screw Tyler. Well, actually that's what I plan to do tonight. Screwing. But with Mr. No Name. The Mr. No Name guy hands Sam his beer just before stepping out of Chaps. "Freckles, will you stop?" I skid to an abrupt halt, but my attention is on the ground now and tears threaten. "What's going on? Is he your boyfriend?"

"What?" I waiver and then shout, "NO! He's a lying, cheating piece of shit."

"Gert!" Mabel yells from behind.

Slowly turning around to my deceiving sister, I begin, "My name is Gertie. Stop calling me Gert! I hate that name and you know it. I've hated it ever since I walked in on him," I point to Tyler, "and saw what he thought of our friendship and love."

"Gertie, please hear me out," Tyler cries. "I have wanted to see you. It's just I've been busy with work and... I love you—"

My hand flies to meet his cheek. "No! You aren't allowed to say that to me anymore." My attention moves to Mabel. "I can't believe you did this." Turning on my heels, I speed-walk faster than ever before to the apartment. Of all times, tomorrow is a huge day, and Mabel pulls this stunt.

Is she the reason he showed up at our apartment this morning? Tears overtake my vision, but I don't need to see where I'm going. I know the way.

$\mathcal{F}$ ive

"All I need to make me happy is a place to sleep at night, a human to bring me food and water, and to give him lots of licks. It makes me want to shred their mattress or pee on their shoes when humans enjoy drama."

~ *Cujo*

Tyler

Wow!

I literally felt the skip my heart made at the sight of her. She's beautiful. The shock of seeing her this morning didn't give me the opportunity to take in her amazing figure. Holy shit, she's even prettier than she was three years ago, and I would have never thought that was possible. Her beauty hypnotizes me.

Wait!

Mabel didn't say she was seeing anyone. What the hell?

Red.

The absolute only fucking color I can see. Then my stomach catches up to my anger filling me with so much regret from my stupid fuck up three years ago. Making a quick detour to the restroom, I vomit the two beers I needed for the courage to face her. Quickly washing up, I return to find the same guy mauling my girl with his tongue. I pull out a stick of gum and begin chewing violently as if it will crush the asshole whose hands are roaming wherever the hell they want. I hope the gum disguises the vomit on my breath because I need to get her away from him and talk. And tell her everything.

How can she allow him to treat her this way? She deserves more than making out on the dance floor. I begin storming toward the two of them when his hand lowers on her abdomen. Mabel is by my side in a blink of an eye. *Dammit.* Why did I think I could do this?

Her eyes are close and it appears she's enjoying the guy slobbering all over her. That was me years ago. It's only ever supposed to be me. Why did I have to drink that night? It changed both of our lives forever. I swore I'd never fuck up again. Standing in front of her watching the two makeout brings fears that I can screw this up in a minute flat.

Finally, she opens her eyes, but the greeting I was expecting is so much different. She looks as if she sees a stranger. Is that what I am? What about what we had?

Is that all I was?

All I ever will be?

I'm not sure if she can understand how much it hurts to see her with someone else. Before I can give it another thought, she turns and runs, grabbing the asshole by the hand on her way out.

I can't let her go again without talking. I have to catch her. "Gert!" I shout praying she'll hear me over the music.

"Who the fuck is that, Mabel? You told me she wasn't seeing anyone," I fire as an explosive wave of fury rips through me following Gert outside with the asshole.

She screams, "She's not. I don't know why she's with him." Her shoulders shrug apologetically.

Our forward movement halts when Gert shouts, "No! He's a lying, cheating piece of shit." Mabel yells something, but I can't make it out.

My heart hurts for the girl I let down. *Dammit!* I was so fucking stupid.

Gertie shouts back. Now I've heard enough. Taking a step forward, I beg for her to hear me out. The sting from her slap reinforces the intense pull my body aches to have. I need her to understand.

The streetlights along with the bar sign illuminate her enough to see her swallow hard and choking back tears. I've hurt her so much. If only she would let me in. But how can you make someone listen to you when you've crushed a dream you painted for them? A dream that for the first time gave them hope for a brighter tomorrow. A tomorrow her parents never got.

Panic fills her eyes and she turns and runs down the sidewalk in the opposite direction. My instincts kick in and I immediately step forward to catch her only to have Mabel stop me.

"Let go!" I yell.

"Tyler, wait. Give her a minute. She just faced you for the second time in years. You can't expect her to just throw her arms around you. Hell, I wanted to kick your ass for the longest time." Mabel points her finger into my chest with the last word.

"I know," I shout throwing my hands in the air. "I'm sorry." I bend over and rest my hands on the tops of my knees. Frustrated, I continue. "I don't know what to do. Please help me talk to her. Get her to listen. It's not just me that needs her," I plead.

"Come on. Let's go back to the apartment." Mabel wraps her arm around me in comfort and I bring her closer. She was always like a sister to me. We didn't spend as much time together as Gert and I had, but I love her. She'll always be family.

Six

"Humans should be more like dogs. Never once have I met a dog that's two-faced."

~ *Cujo*

Gertie

Reaching for the door, another hand is quicker. Turning around in a fog, I find Mr. No Name. He opens the door and motions for me to go ahead. Silently, I do. and we remain quiet as he pushes the elevator button. He follows me into the moving box and I hold up two fingers for him to push for the second floor. The door closes and I can feel his eyes on me. I look up to confirm my thoughts. He's staring. At me. Before the elevator comes to a stop on my floor, he moves closer until he's so close we're almost touching. And then he presses his body into mine causing me to yelp as my back hits the wall. There's a heavy jolt and the motherfucking elevator is stuck again, but my attention is too consumed to care or worry that I'm claustrophobic.

Mr. No Name moves his head down until our lips touch and, oh, my God... passion erupts. The kiss turns feverish and we both can't get enough. "Freckles," he whispers as our lips pull away shortly for air. Instinctively, my hands reach up pulling his hair so that his lips are back on mine. I need them. I want them to make me forget. He groans and I push my hips back against his. Holy shit he has me all tied up. He lifts my legs to wrap around his waist and pushes me against the elevator wall. The heady moment has me clinging onto his body. There is no telling where my hands roam, my mind is not in control of them. My head lifts toward the ceiling. The moment is too intense. His warm lips find my neck kissing and licking their way to uncharted territory. With his hands on my rear, he grinds his excitement into my ache, which has me sighing and moaning. "God, Freckles, I want you so bad..." he whispers with his hot breath on my ear. I moan again, wanting more. My fingers tighten in his hair begging for his lips again. "How long has it been?" he asks.

Wait, what?

My fingers immediately pause. "How long what?"

"Since you've been with another man?" His throaty voice doesn't remove the coldness I feel remembering ass-hat back at the pub. I drop my legs and push him back.

"I... uh... I can't do this." His stare goes through me and I swear it touches my conscience.

"Why not? Just a minute ago, you were ready for me to strip you and take you right here against the wall." A shiver flows through my veins at that thought. *But then there is...*

"I'm sorry—"

"Hello? Anyone in there?" A man's voice shouts from below. Shit! The fire department.

"Yes!" I shout wanting to get out of here and behind my bedroom door.

"This is Harris Fire Department, and we'll have you out as soon as possible. Are you alone, ma'am?" Damn, how long were we making out? The fire department normally takes fifteen minutes to arrive. It all went by too quickly. *Ugh.*

My eyes burn from Mr. No Name's stare. "Ma'am?" *Oh, shit.*

"Umm… no, there is a gentleman in here, too." Mr. No Name bridges the gap between us.

"I'd love nothing more than to show you how wrong you are by calling me a gentleman." My eyebrows draw together in confusion. "I don't want to be a gentleman, Freckles. I want to fuck your brains out and watch you come all night." I gasp, and suddenly, I'm speechless. For someone who is an editor, you'd think I'd have words to respond to that. But no. He sucked them away along with all my modesty. My eyes water and I quickly look away shaking my head. "Let me take your mind off him. I can make you forget. I'm not asking for anything in return. Just one night." His voice becomes demanding.

"I'm sorry, I can't—" The elevator jolts again as it begins to ascend, and my hands reach out for the walls to brace myself to only land on thick muscles. I'm done with today and all the movements that are teetering my balance.

We must have been at my floor because the doors almost immediately open revealing a few heavily dressed firemen, Mabel, Tyler, and friends.

Jumping back and away from the guy, whose name I should know before I do acts such as this, I square my shoulders and lift my chin. Yeah, I'm *so* done with today.

"What the hell?" Tyler quips. My eyes narrow and I battle my way through the melee and past all of them and their stares. I hear Mr. No Name call out 'Freckles' while chuckling from behind and Mabel begins to yell at him. I don't care. Tyler's shouting is going to wake the entire building. Commotion erupts. I quickly unlock the apartment, tempted to bolt and chain it from the inside, but decide to make a run for my room where I will be safe.

Seven

"I am not aggressive or vicious. I'm merely protecting my human."

~ *Cujo*

Tyler

"What the hell?" I somehow manage after watching Gert pull away from asshole. She gives me a look that could kill and pushes past us. Asshole decides this moment to call her 'Freckles' like a fucking pet.

"Why the fuck are you calling her Freckles? She has a name, Asshole." I lunge forward slamming him against the back of the elevator wall. His 'humph' was enough to tell me he wasn't expecting it.

"Tyler!" Mabel shouts snapping me out of my rage. Shit! I turn around just as the firemen begin to yank me off the bastard.

"I'm good," I voice to those thinking this asshole deserves to keep his pretty face. *Dammit.* I didn't come here to cause shit like this. I need to talk to Gert and have her hear me out. I'm not expecting planets to realign or someone to find a cure for cancer because, *dammit,* that would make so many people sleep better at night. Me being one of them. I just need five minutes.

Will I ever be able to make this right?

Asshole stands cocky wearing his smug grin and it takes everything I have in me to turn and walk away. Heading for the stairs where I had run up only moments ago, I fight to keep moving. My heart tells me to go fight Gertie's stubbornness. My head is telling me that will only make things worse. I need to give her some time.

Time.

People take that word and its worth for granted every day.

Pushing the door to the stairwell open, I run out of her building hoping I can make it to the hotel before I beat the shit out of something or someone.

One step in the quiet, lonely room, I slide down the closed door and put my head in my hands. My life is a mess and I don't see how I can possibly fix this.

If I can't get Gert to listen to me, I'll be letting so many people down... and that's just not acceptable.

I have to figure something out.

And soon.

Eight

"The bones were in my reach. How was I supposed to know he didn't want me to have them? If only I came with instructions, Mr. Prissy Pants wouldn't be so irritable."

~ *Cujo*

Gertie

"Gertie?" Voices envelop my room from the other side of the door holding my sunken form where I fell once it closed. I'd like nothing more than to close myself off to the world, but thanks to the thin walls, I can't drown out the echo of voices. Tears fall freely. I haven't seen him in three years. Why does it hurt so badly to see his face, to hear his voice, or to even feel the touch of his skin when I slapped him?

Lowering my head into my hands, I wonder what Tyler could possibly want to tell me. Why is he here after all this time? Do I want to know? More importantly, do I have the strength to listen and stand my ground? *Ugh!* I have an awesome job that I need to be ready for tomorrow.

This is so not fair. And then Mr. No Name. Seriously? One night? There is no way on God's green earth that I could do that. And Mabel, she betrayed my trust and me. Now I know why she was so excited to get to Chaps. Well, I won't be going out with her anytime soon. *If ever.*

I stand to change into a t-shirt and shorts. I try to ignore Mabel crying for everyone to leave. I don't want to deal with her, but I need to go into the room next to mine. Listening for the front door to close, I swing open my bedroom door and rush to the bathroom where I can close yet another door and lock it. Tears continue to fall as the emotions come flying back as if I walked in on Tyler and the town tramp only yesterday. I gave him everything. All of me. How can I ever trust a man again? Lost in thought, I finish washing and open the door before a crying Mabel falls back. She must have been leaning against the door.

"Gertie." I curtly raise my hand to stop her while I step by. "Please, I'm sorry. I'm so sorry, Gert…ie. I never meant—"

I close my bedroom door before she finishes. I can tell she's sorry, but what she doesn't realize is how much seeing him hurts. It's as if she forgot everything that he had done to me. Or perhaps dismissed it all. Whatever the reason, I don't care right now. Tomorrow is bound to be a long day and I didn't need this bullshit tonight.

Sliding into my soft sheets, I reach over and set 'the monster' also known as my alarm clock, for five in the morning. A head start is just what I need tomorrow. Falling onto my pillow, I stare at the ceiling as my head spins. A one-night stand? Who the hell does that? Do relationships not mean anything anymore? Rolling over, I clench the sheets and close my eyes.

Movements in the kitchen tell me Mabel isn't sitting at my door anymore. *Thank heavens.* My phone vibrates and I pray it isn't Grammy. *Oh, hell no!* She did not call in the bulldog, Rick. Quickly turning off my phone, I toss it into my side table drawer where my eyes catch sight my little friend. *Well, dayum.* Mr. No Name *did* leave me with an ache that needs releasing.

I close my eyes while thoughts of us dancing tonight begin to warm my blood. *Freckles.* I might like that he calls me Freckles. It felt so good to have someone want me like that. And he was excited, too. His cock pressed against me promising a healthy size that could do naughty things. Fuck, maybe I should have taken him up on his offer. My hips move as I picture us in the elevator with him grinding against me. Pressure builds while I move my little friend around, pushing a higher setting. His mouth. Oh, those lips. Joy to the world! My other hand traces the lips he tasted, nibbled, and made sore. My release is coming. It's so close. Mr. No Name was so fucking sexy and maybe elevator sex would have been awesome had the doors not opened to expose Tyler standing there.

Cold.

Nothing.

No hope for this going further.

Dammit! That ass-hat just took one more thing away from me. Fuck him!

Tossing my little friend back into the drawer, I sit in bed knowing I won't be having pleasant dreams tonight. There will be no choosing to be the future Mrs. Adam Levine.

No, two men tainted my thoughts.

Tyler.

Mr. No Name.

Fuck the male population. I'm done.

No more Freckles!

Nine

"If only humans would lick their paws and get over stupid shit. It's like crap, so don't eat it. That's what the humans do. Eating the bullshit that was fed to them. If the humans let things go, everyone would be much happier, including me. This drama is seriously interrupting my afternoon nap. They need to learn how to play dead, for heaven's sake."

~ Cujo

Gertie

The mile walk to the office is as predictable as always. Rushed, panicked drivers on the road inching their way closer and closer to their destination with the sense that their life is more important than others. It not only infuriates me that people are so simple minded, but it can also be entertaining.

A mile might seem long to walk to work, but Mabel chose the apartment building because of its proximity. Almost exactly half way from both of our offices. I like it because it gives me an opportunity to get some exercise in the morning and in the evening. It would probably take me just as long to get here if I drove. Oh, but then I'd need a car and remember, I don't like to spend needlessly. I have everything I need within walking distance. If I have to travel, there are taxi cabs, buses, trains, and planes. So why not walk and get lost in the song streaming through my earbuds?

The bitter morning breeze is hardly refreshing but helps me keep my mind off a few things. My warm liquid breakfast helps bite back the shiver. Slacks, a pretty blouse and large overflowing sweater are my 'meet the new boss' attire. Although, I'm sure these tennis shoes will not earn a great impression, but the black with red accents Christian Louboutin shoes that are secured in my backpack are sure to remedy the situation. I guess I may have left out that I tend to splurge on shoes in addition to my bed sheets. Well, then there are my clothes because, let's face it, I have to create an impression. I don't always dress like this though. I have fashion sense, only I possess a style that is me. When I'm not in work attire, shorts and flip-flops have my heart. I'd prefer them over all this other *hoity-toity* crap any day, but I'm an adult and have to at least look the part.

Tossing my sunglasses among the heap of papers already littering my desk, I flop into my chair and pull out my perfume to get rid of the smell of outside. Don't laugh or question me. There is such a thing as someone smelling like outside for a period of time. I'm not talking about people who don't wear deodorant. I'm talking about the distinct smell one wears after being outside and I prefer not to wear it.

Well, this morning has really started out wrong. First, the monster screamed so loud it may have awakened people in Canada. Then I avoided Mabel like the plague and my sunglasses did little to relieve the sun burning my tired, puffy eyes. I had to spend extra time with them this morning to help reduce the swelling. Great, I'm meeting my new boss looking like crap. I suppose that's what I get for allowing everything to come crashing down where I cried myself to sleep.

"Hi, Gertie," Penny, my secretary, greets a little too cheerfully walking into my office as I fire up my laptop.

Mondays.

They should be illegal everywhere. Particularly when you have a sister like Mabel.

"Uh, oh. What happened to you?" Penny questions. She is a sweetheart and one of those girls that everyone loves. The world will come to an end before she harms a fly. *Literally.* I become consumed in my own thoughts.

Mr. No Name. Thank God, I didn't run into him. Not that I ever saw him before. So, why would I even worry about running into him? Oh, dear, I'm rambling in my head now. I have no interest in seeing him anytime in the future, for that matter. Likewise, I don't want to hear the word freckles either. See the drama that goes along with guys, relationships, and all that shit? I don't need that crap. Tyler was more than enough. *Tyler.* What a douchebag thinking he can come back into my life after all this time. Please God, have him go back to whatever hole he crawled out so I don't have to deal with him. How could Mabel tell him where we live? *Mabel*. I drop my head into my hands and moan. Why did I listen to her and go to Chaps? If only I had put my foot down, none of the events last night would've occurred.

"Uh, Gertie?" Penny audibly plops herself in the leather seat in front of my desk. "You know…"

My right hand flies down onto the desk. "Yes, I know, Penny." I can't help but rub my throbbing temples hoping to ease some of the discomforts before meeting what might turn out to be my new nightmare. No positive vibes here. Penny's shocked gasp has me opening my eyes in horror. "Oh, my gosh, I'm so sorry I snapped at you. It's just…"

She just shakes her head. "I came in here to say hi and… and…" Oh, hell, *not* the tears. I'm a certifiable bitch.

Promptly, I walk around my desk to pull her into a hug. "I'm so sorry, Penny. I never meant to snap at you. My nerves are shot and after last night, I don't know what to think." I rub her back trying to fix her mood. Geez, I need to pull myself together so that I don't lash out at others. "I'm truly sorry and will try my best to never do that again. Okay?" She nods. "Hurting you was never my intention. Forgive me?" I ask hopefully.

Pulling away, she swats my shoulder. "Oh, stop it. I'm just a bundle of nerves right now. I have never handled new situations well and even took a nerve pill to get me through today."

My nose scrunches. "You had to take a nerve pill? Sweetie, that can't be good." Damn, she's *only* a secretary at best. I do most of the work myself. How can this be so stressful that she needs to take a nerve pill? Now, had I been smart, this would be a red flag, but I never claimed to be anything other than of average intellect.

"Yeah, it's just Darwin is getting on my nerves. I wish the season would begin so he'd go back to doing lawn care already. I had a horrible migraine this weekend, and I constantly worried about meeting Rachel. You know, I want her to like me." She retreats to the chair, sinking her larger figure into it and immediately reaching over to grab a tissue off the table next to her. I sit down in an unoccupied seat on the opposite side of the table hoping my calm demeanor will help her nerves. Because, dayum, I had no idea about her nerve issues. She's been my secretary for almost a year now. Well, that doesn't make me feel better. I sway my head, disgusted with myself.

"I'm sorry for breaking down." Penny continues to carry on while dabbing her eyes.

"No troubles. And you have absolutely nothing to worry about with Rachel. Everyone loves you and I'm certain she's going to, as well. In fact, I can guarantee it. You really have nothing to worry about. Chin up, love." I finish reassuring her before proceeding to my usual space behind the desk and getting my head in the game.

"Thanks, Gertie. I'll see you in a bit."

"You, too," I quip not bothering to take my eyes off the screen in front of me. I need to go through my emails and… there's an email from my new boss, Rachel. I take a deep breath and open it.

From: Rachel Dumascus
Date: Monday, 3 March 2014 6:49 A.M.
To: Rachel Dumascus Editing and Writing Team
Subject: Introductions

Good morning, Ladies and Gentlemen.

I look forward to meeting you all. Please arrive no later than 9:00 A.M. in the Fashion Conference Room.

Regards,

Rachel Dumascus
Head Editor-in-Chief
Simple Luxury
Houston, TX

The Fashion Conference Room? *Great... Not!* That means I have to pass Jennifer's desk. We used to be close, but I had to put some distance between us. Once she opened up about both of her son's disabilities, which wasn't the first thing out of her mouth, but closely followed, it seemed like that was all she talked about. She's in the fashion division and her head needs to get out of her ass, so to speak, because it is a big ass. Crap, Gram's coming out of me again. I feel terrible for what her sons are going through, but she works it to her advantage to gather friends, acceptance (for what, I don't know) and throws her weight with the rest of the writing team. I don't play games like that. That's just dirty. Shit like that really pisses me off.

Glancing at the bottom corner, I check the time on my laptop. *Whew.* I have thirty more minutes. My attention returns to other emails. There is one from Rick and Mabel.

Rolling my eyes, I decide to hold off reading Mabel's for later, but click on Rick's email instead.

From: Rick the Dick
Date: Sunday, 2 March 2014 11:28 P.M.
To: Gertie Sawyer
Subject: WTF?

The subject speaks for itself. What the fuck happened tonight, and why aren't you answering my phone calls or texts? You made me resort to email. And you know how much I fucking hate email. So pick up the phone, gorgeous and call my pretty ass!

Don't make me have to come down there. I'll bring Cujo.

Smoochies,

Rick the Dick
Your Latin Lover

I laugh simply because of the name I assigned him in my address book. When I told him I was going to name him Rick the Dick, he got all sappy and said he wouldn't believe it until he saw it. He jumped up and down, fanning himself acting like a teenage girl after I pushed my phone in his face the last time he visited. Oh, dear, he's coming to visit this weekend. Rick can be a bit of a diva.

I quickly send a reply that I'll call him later if I have time. Telling him that I have a lot of work to do will keep him sufficed for now. He knows how serious I take my work and luckily, I can use it to my advantage since I have no life except for Free Friday. My one night to let loose with three of my best friends. April, Leslie, Mindy, and I have been friends since we hit it off in college. Now that we've taken on responsible roles after graduation, we've dedicated Friday for our weekly fun. We call it Free Friday. Two simple rules. No drama and no guys. It's just us girls. Although we've allowed Rick to tag along a couple of times. But he doesn't count.

After responding to a few other emails, I close my inbox and shut down my laptop. I don't know what Mabel could say that would make this any better. I hope she'll be meeting co-workers for cocktails after work so I don't have to see her. How can someone spend so much time partying and having fun? The bigger question is, how can she be such an exceptional writer when she barely concentrates on her career? Working for a prestigious magazine, she highlights developmental economic crap. And they call *me* boring? *Pfft! Whatever.* Perhaps that's what drives her to drink.

Everything appears to be in order here. I stand and gather my files ready to meet the new boss.

The stark, cold Fashion Conference Room is where writers, editors, and all of their assistants will soon join together like a herd of buffalo packing together as if wolf predation was present. Luckily, I am one of the first to arrive and can pick my usual seat.

Moments later, seats begin to fill around the conference table as everyone waves, shakes hands, or nods to their co-workers. Thankfully, we all understand we don't have to be best friends. Penny takes her seat next to me leaving the one to my left empty. Looking around, I take attendance wondering who will be... *no!* Shoot, I get to have the wonderful Jennifer sit next to me. Great. Why not have her sit there and make the last twenty-four hours even better?

"Hi, Gertie." She plasters a fake smile that makes me cringe, but instead, has me reciprocating the phonies. The last thing I want is Rachel walking in witnessing me giving Jennifer a dose of reality true-bitch style. "How was your weekend?" she continues our one-sided conversation.

Penny elbows me playfully, knowing I can't stand Jennifer. "Mine was great," I lie adding, "You should ask Penny what she did. I heard she had an amazing weekend." I move around to wink at my evil secretary.

Lucky for Penny, our new boss walks in saving her from answering. "Good morning, everyone." Rachel greets me and my peers. "I'm very excited to be here. I'd like to tell you a little bit of my background to familiarize you with my past. I was sixth in my graduating class of Sanford ten years ago. Immediately moving to New York, I caught a break working for this company at their headquarters. I didn't get my start as an editor or a writer. No, I was an assistant so I desire you all to understand education means a lot to me, but so does your work ethic. If you work hard, we're going to get along great, but if you give me mediocre crap, start making a cardboard sign for when I kick your ass to the curb." She pauses. "So that's everything in a nutshell. I understand things run in a certain lackadaisical manner before I arrived. Please realize that is no longer the case from this point forward. Corporate brought me here to push this office in the growing direction they once had. If this doesn't work, there will be a hostile takeover and you all will be on the streets regardless with your cardboard signs. Shareholders have an invested interest and corporate will not disappoint them." Shit, I reckon I'm going shopping for a new wardrobe if I have to dress like this all the time. It would seem ridiculous if I came to the office in the same two outfits. It would be like a prison suit or uniform. Oh, wouldn't that give Jennifer something else to talk about? Rachel claps her hands as if she's ready to get down to the *nitty-gritty* right now. *Wait, a hostile takeover?*

"That's all I have to say at the moment. Just know, work hard—you're good, don't pull your weight and excel—you're gone." She places her hands on her hips looking around. "Mark, my assistant, will be in touch. I want to have a meeting with the writing and editing teams, as well as the assistants, individually, but I don't have time right now. Meeting adjourned."

My leg bounces as I nervously wonder if I should start looking at employment sites. I'm a hard worker, I go above and beyond... Uh-oh. Rachel's eyes land on mine, and she immediately speaks. "Ms. Sawyer, I'd like to have a word with you." Oh, shit, here it goes. I'm gonna get fired. Done. *Fuckity, fuck, fuck.* Penny walks behind Rachel on her way out mouthing 'I'm sorry.' Jennifer turns her head just as she walks out and smirks. Oh, that fucking fake bitch is going to get what's coming to her. *Shit!* Oh, what does it matter? I'm the one who was called out of everyone else to stay behind.

As soon as the last body leaves, Rachel stands up to close the conference room door while I sit glued to my seat sweating profusely. I wonder if the smell of outside is sweat residue. If so, I'm sure I reek of it. Rachel walks around the other side, allowing her long manicured nails to run along of the conference table. Almost as irritating as a chalkboard. Damn, I feel like I'm in the principal's office. She stops directly across the table, resting her palms flat and leans forward. I swallow hard. *No... that was a gulp.*

"Ms. Sawyer, the reason I kept you behind is I've had the privilege to review your file already." *Oh, shoot. What's in there? Fuckity, fuck, fuck.* I've never been *privileged* to a file. "Relax, Gertie. I was shocked by your achievements. Based on what I read in your file, you remind me of myself. Therefore, I wanted to speak to you in private. According to my findings, you excel and manage to gather stories many never will. Now, Simple Luxury is about just that. Simple. Luxury." Her 'p' popped and 'luxury' rolled off her tongue as if it were a creamy chocolate mousse dessert. Oh, I could go for chocolate right about now. An entire conference table full of nothing but rich, creamy chocolate. *Hmm...*

"So how does that sound?" *Crap.* What sound? Oh no! What the hell did I *just* miss?

"Umm, great." Dammit, I can't go asking her what she meant now and not look like a complete incompetent dumbass.

Her face lights up. "Wonderful. It will only be for three days." *Wait, what?* Think Gertie, think.

"So, will my secretary need to handle travel arrangements?" That's a great question to have her spill the beans. Right?

"Oh, heavens, no. I already knew you would say yes, so we're booked on a morning flight next Tuesday." The air escapes my lungs. She already knew I would say yes? Am I really that predictable? That's probably better than being considered boring.

"Okay." My fingers lock themselves together in my lap. "Is there anything I need to prepare for the trip?" Please tell me. Please, please don't realize I wasn't listening.

"You are well versed already. I have no doubt you'll get exactly what we discussed." She walks to the exit slowly turning toward me just before she disappears. "I don't believe you have to worry for one second about losing your job. Don't prove me wrong." She leaves without as much as a goodbye. What the *fuck* did we discuss?

Gathering my files along with my crumbled nerves, I step out of the Fashion Conference Room and past an unhappy Jennifer speaking with Rachel. *Humph.* Jennifer's eyes no doubt traveled down to my shoes. Of course, I smirk. That's a real no-brainer. Another no-brainer? I love my shoes.

Ten

"I need to meditate. All this drama is just too much for one dog to handle."

~ *Cujo*

Tyler

The ceiling hasn't changed one bit over the last few hours. Perhaps I should get up and face the fact I've lost my chance to ask Gert for forgiveness and tell her why I'm here.

Rolling over onto my stomach, I hide my head in the pillow. My God, she's gorgeous. Every single feeling for her intensified the moment her eyes met mine. How do I walk away from someone who owns most of my heart? Everything seems small and miniscule compared to her. I thought I could fix this.

Dammit, I've been chasing after her ghost for so long, I don't know what to do next. Maybe I should just go home and finally let her go. As difficult as it is to walk away, it might be what she needs. It just might be the hardest thing I'll ever have to do, but I'll do anything for her. I love her so fucking much.

I grip the pillow hard and hug it. My heart is tearing apart. I finally see my girl and I have to walk away.

Fucking tears. For the love of God, I *am* a pansy.

My cell phone chimes receiving a text message.

Mabel: It might be best if you go home. I'm sorry things didn't work out.

I stare at her text wanting the events of last night to be a nightmare.

Me: I know. I'm heading back.

With that, I toss my phone across the room furious over the situation. A situation I created. A situation I can't fix or control right now. My fists repeatedly pound into the mattress, the victim of my emotions.

"Why?" I cry helplessly to no one in particular. Damn, I should probably pray. Maybe God will help Gert and me.

I can't leave without saying goodbye. The need to see her at least one more time is overwhelming.

Determination settles in. I'm going to try again. I have to, but first I have to call Mom.

Jumping out of bed, I reach for the phone hoping it still works. Sure enough. At least something is going for me. I take a much-needed deep breath before dialing as I settle against the headboard.

"Hey, sweetheart." I roll my eyes at Mom's greeting. I'm how old and she addresses me as she did when I was in kindergarten.

"Hi, Ma. How are things?"

"Great. You know everything is just fine. I have a handle on it. You just concentrate on bringing your girl home."

"Ma, I messed up."

"Sweetheart, don't worry. I have faith you will find a way back into her heart."

"But, Ma, she still hates me."

"I doubt she hates you. That girl loved you with every fiber of her being growing up. Before the two of you went from just friends to a more intimate relationship, I knew one day you'd be together. Trust me. She doesn't hate you. I'm sure she was just shocked seeing you after all this time and reached out for the easiest emotion."

"Well, we were together and then I fucked up."

"Excuse me?" Ma questions irritated.

"Sorry, Ma. But, she's so angry. You could see it all over her face." I sigh and close my eyes wanting to hide from the heartache.

"I hope you're not giving up."

"Ma, I can't cause her anymore pain by being here."

"Tyler Allen Jackson, you need to grow a pair." I gasp forgetting how abrupt Ma can be. She doesn't mince words. "Don't sit there and tell me you expected me to say anything else." Damn, the old woman's right. I needed her reassurance that I was doing the right thing.

"I plan to try one more time tonight. If nothing else, just to say goodbye," I confess.

"And what about—"

"I don't know, Ma. I'll give it another shot. If that doesn't work, I need to leave her alone."

"Okay, good luck, sweetheart. I love you."

"I love you too. Can you give—" She cuts me off.

"Already done." I'm so thankful to have my mom.

"Ma, you don't know how much I appreciate this."

"I know you do. Go get your Gert."

"Okay. Bye."

"Bye, sweetheart." I hang up after Ma's last word.

Falling to the side, thoughts begin to swarm my head. Shit. I told Mabel I was leaving. Do I tell her I'm stopping by tonight? *Hell, no.* I can't have anyone messing this up or interfering.

Can she forgive me after all this time? I guess we'll have to wait and see. First, I need to go over some accounts and make sure proposals and permits are all in order. Pulling out my laptop, I try to immerse myself in work and hope tonight works itself out.

Monday's are always crazy thanks to lazy-ass people who take off work early on Friday to only play catch up on the following Monday mornings.

By ten o'clock, I have the entire permit shit from last week resolved and job sites appear to be in order. Now, I have time to work on the final design touches of the house I built. I don't think I'll ever leave Eufaula. There are too many memories to walk away from. They are all I hold right now. Not sure if I'll survive without them.

I'm pretty excited about the progress my crew is making on one of the sites—a two-story country home with a wraparound porch that will, in time, hold a swing like Dad and Ma have. The lot sits closer to Gram than she originally cared for, but after my year of purgatory she told me how ecstatic she is. Once the house is inspected and cleared, I will begin working on the dock. I have something special in mind and can't have anyone else touch the job.

Until then, I'll try not to think about tonight. Or her.

But I'd be lying to myself.

She's *all* I can think about.

All I dream about.

I'm so fucking screwed.

Eleven

"Why would humans rather be unhappy apart, than to just get it over with and be together? I mean, if there is a vacant inch on the sofa, my hind quarters will find it. Ask Mr. Prissy Pants, he knows!"

~ *Cujo*

Gertie

I slap the files down on the desk, sit in my chair, and spin around in circles with my eyes closed, trying to think what I'm going to do. I need to find out what the hell I agreed to, shop for a larger wardrobe, deal with Mabel, and then Rick. Oh, and pray I never run into Tyler again.

My phone rings. "Yes?" I ask after reaching blindly for the speaker button.

"I have a gentleman requesting to speak with you on line one," Penny informs.

Opening my eyes to look at the speaker as if it's *not* an inanimate object, I ask, "Did he say who he was with?"

"Um.." Penny hesitates.

Seriously, Penny? Do your effing job! Ugh, I hate micromanaging people. Sitting up, I shake off the previous conflict of thoughts.

"Never mind, I've got it." I sigh. "Could you bring me a glass of water, please?" I hate asking her to get stuff that I'm very capable of handling myself, but I have to take this call.

Clearing my throat, I pick up the line. "This is Gertie Sawyer."

"Yes, hello, Ms. Sawyer. I am calling to ask how the transition with Ms. Damascus is going." *Huh?*

"I just had the privilege of meeting her. What did you say your name was again?"

"I didn't." Silence. "I made sure your secretary has my information should you need it." Click. *What the fuck?* With the phone still up to my ear, I sit dumbfounded by what had just happened.

Penny walks in carrying my glass of water. Her face morphs when she recognizes my stupor. "Gertie?"

"Who was that on the phone? He said you had his information if I need it," I drill her irritated at her lack of work ethic for me.

"Yes, but he demanded that I not give it to you." She looks down at her feet.

"But, what if I need it, Penny?" I'm confused.

"He assured me he'll tell me when you need it." She finishes softly.

I draw my eyebrows together. "What the *fuck* does that mean?"

"Knock, knock." Rachel walks in. *Shit!* She just witnessed me cussing. *Fuckity, fuck, fuck!* My seated body doesn't react. I'm ready to be canned. "Gertie, would you like to grab lunch with me?" *Oh, am I'm not getting fired?*

"Uh… let me look at my…"

"There is nothing on your calendar." Penny chose *now* to do her job.

"Then it's settled," Rachel declares, walking out the door.

I'm lost and confused. Throwing my head in my hands, I go over the events of the day and how fucking strange everything is. *Not strange.* Weird! It's as if I've gone into the cosmos of the Twilight Zone.

"Oh, and I have some files on the article Rachel wants you to work on when you travel to Washington, DC next week," Penny explains.

"Washington, DC? What's in Washington? Am I meeting the President?" My eyes grow at the possibility.

Penny laughed. "No, silly. And if that ever happens, you had better take me. Don't you know you're going to one of the largest writer's conventions and it's exclusive to only the top ten nationally recognized magazines?" She stares at me. "Uh, hello? MEW Con, Gertie!"

My face lights up. "Are you serious?" I jump up suddenly giddy from the best news ever.

"Didn't Rachel already explain this?" Penny questions confused.

"Well, perhaps. I sort of got distracted in the meeting and missed part of our conversation." I sheepishly shrug.

"Young lady, you need to quit having those squirrel moments or who knows what could happen," Penny scolds. *Blah, blah, blah.* I internally roll my eyes.

"Whatever. So where in DC is this convention being held?"

A smile grows on her face. "DAR Headquarters."

With eyes bugging out, I ask, "You mean DAR as in Daughters of the American Revolution?" She nods her head. "Sweet! I haven't been in such a long time." I sigh. "It feels like a phone call to Gram is in order." I just need to pray to the almighty God that she doesn't find a way to attend herself. Knowing Gram, anything is possible. Maybe I should hold off mentioning it until after the trip.

"Oh, she is going to be so envious. How long has she had you and Mabel involved?"

Resting my head against the back of my chair, I glance at the ceiling to think. "I believe we were eighteen when we were allowed to join our local chapter. It's fun and you meet interesting people at the numerous events, but..." I don't finish.

My inevitable lunch date arrives. "Ready?" Rachel asks after knocking twice.

"Yes," sitting up straighter I turn back to my computer, "let me send this and we can go."

The walk is short to the quaint little bistro where I suggested we grab a bite. My sweaty palms are a big indicator of how nervous I am to share the same air with this woman. Small talk over our college days helped to break the ice while we ate. I chose my usual salad because this girl does not exercise—except for the mile to and from work. Our apartment complex has a state of the art fitness room, but my fat ass would rather work than exercise. Seriously, whom do I have to impress? As I nibble on my tree leaves, Rachel sinks her teeth into a sandwich that from the looks of it is going to add ten pounds straight to my midriff. *Lovely.*

Rachel interrupts my inner thoughts. "You know," she begins, "never in my lifetime did I imagine I'd be a big time editor-in-chief. I've always wanted to be a writer. Seriously, who the hell wants all that responsibility? I thought I'd be sitting in front of a boring monitor all day." She pauses, giving me a moment to gather myself from her shocking revelation. "Whoever said the research and that writing was easy is a moron." I sit mummified at how open she is with me. "I mean, Harold didn't understand why I had to work longer hours, even though it was my paycheck supporting him." *Who the hell is Harold?* "He wanted me home and didn't want to know about my day or any of the exciting stories I was privileged to write. Therefore, you see, Gertie, this is why I see so much of myself in you. Work is your number one priority in life and that is what is going to allow you to make it far in this industry. And yes, I can tell all of this by reading your file. Your performance over the last two years is astonishing and the fact that bozo didn't promote you earlier or give you bigger stories shows it was time for him to leave the company." Oh, wow. How courteous of her to talk down about my former boss. I mean, yeah, sure. A great deal of what I did went unrecognized, but I didn't do it for that. I did my job. I hold high expectations of myself and won't complete anything half-assed.

"We should go out for drinks one night this week," Rachel says on our way back into the office. *Excuse me?*

"Um, are you sure?" I ask. First of all, I don't like to drink much, party, or shit like that. Second, isn't there some code where you don't mix business with pleasure?

"Of course, silly! Here, let me see your phone." She snatches it out of my hand before I can protest. "There, I put my contact information in there and then called my phone. Now we have each other's number. If you need anything, just call." I don't respond. There isn't any point to retort because she's already walking away—allowing me to stand here and mull over what exactly had just occurred.

Twelve

"Oh, dear, God, no! Mr. Prissy Pants says I need a bath. Says I played in the mud. I have no idea what he's talking about. The mud came out of nowhere and just landed on me. Maybe cute puppy eyes will make him change his mind."

~ *Cujo*

Gertie

Five o'clock rolls around and I can't get out of this weird place fast enough. I'd rather deal with Mabel than this crazy shit. I have three friends. I don't need any others... and most certainly not my boss. Mabel's friends are hers, and I enjoy hanging out with them sometimes, but I need my down time from work. *Ambitious, yes, I know.* Down time isn't supposed to be fulfilled with work, but whatever. Haven't you already figured me out? I work. Period.

Pulling out my cell phone after changing into my tennis shoes, I come across a text from Mabel.

Mabel: You here?

Gertie: No

Mabel: We need to talk.

Gertie: No

Mabel: I'M SORRY GERTIE!

I ignore her and put my earbuds in instead of responding. Laptop, files, and heels are packed. Slipping on my sweater, I swing my backpack over my shoulders and begin the mile with the inaugural tone. With the first step, I pull my sweater tighter. My phone dings in my ear.

Mabel: Come on. Please don't hate me.

She *didn't* just say that. I never could bring myself to hate her. Not with everything we've been through together. She and Gram are my only family. And this is why I can't stay mad at her or tell her no.

Gertie: It's fine. Make sure he's gone. I never want to see him again. I could never hate you, honey.

Mabel: He went home last night. I promise. Love you.

Gertie: Luv you more.

Oh, thank the heavens!

The evening air is warmer than earlier, thanks to the bright sun that surprisingly doesn't bother my eyes anymore. There is still a chill in the air, but it's tolerable. The surrounding buildings act as a shield against the wind, keeping me protected.

I refuse to allow another night like last to happen again. I'm going home to change before I begin my shopping spree. I wish the cute boutiques were on this side of the apartment and I could catch one on my way.

Reaching the apartment, I say a couple of Hail Marys that tonight will be uneventful. The trip up to the second level is a lot calmer than last nights. Mabel immediately pulls me into a hug when I step inside. "I'm so sorry, Gertie. Please. I didn't mean to hurt you." I hug her back knowing she was only trying to do something nice. "I thought maybe..." she pulls back to look me in the eye, "maybe, after all this time, you two could..." I shake my head stopping her. "Gertie, he was your best friend. You can't just throw that away. He's like a brother to you." My eyes grow. "Okay, that's sort of rank since you two did become an item." We laugh lightening the mood.

"Mabel, I don't want to go through all the drama involved in a relationship. Last night was proof that I'm not over what happened with Tyler. I don't think I necessarily grieve the loss of our intimate connection, but it's the friendship. We did practically everything together. I miss the boy who taught me to tie my shoes or who threw spitballs across the classroom into my hair because he wanted to tease me. I miss the boy who taught me how to drive a stick shift and the one who was there for me every year on that day. He was there when—" I can't finish. Tears streamed down both of our cheeks.

Mabel moves my hair behind my ears and out of my face. "Gertie, that guy is still there. He just made a stupid mistake." I nod my head.

"I know you are merely looking out for me. It's all okay. Tyler and I are over though. I can't do it again,

Mabel." I wipe the moisture from my face. "I do have something you can help me with, though." Her eyes light up. Taking a step back to wipe her own face, she waits. "I met my new boss today."

"Oh, how is she?"

Slinging my backpack off and kicking my shoes to the side, I answer, "Interesting." With Mabel's quizzical look, I continue. "I don't know where to begin. Let's see," I walk into the kitchen to get a glass of water and, after a sip, I lean my hip against the counter and continue, "I need to go shopping tonight and get a couple of outfits. I'm expected to wear pretty shit like this," I motion down my figure, "all the time."

"Gertie, you are pretty. You looked beautiful today. Well, except for your raccoon eyes." She laughs and I slap her.

"That's your fault for doing the whole big bear hug when I walked into the door." She rolls her eyes. "I found out I'm traveling to Washington, DC next Tuesday for three days. Oh, my gosh, you'll never believe where I'm going!"

"Well... spill it already," she retorts irritated that I needed another sip of water.

"DAR Headquarters for MEW Con. You know, the writers convention that's exclusive to only the top ten nationally recognized magazines?" I smile, and we both jump up and down holding onto each other.

"Holy shit, Gertie. That's pretty fucking amazing actually. How did you land that opportunity?"

"I don't know. Rachel seems nice. We had a meeting and she wound up keeping me after to tell me about a trip that she targeted me to attend with her. It's all just so strange. And she pretends like she's my new best friend."

Mabel scrunches her nose in confusion.

"Maybe I'm wrong, but it makes me uncomfortable. She asked me to lunch where she proceeded to ask me to tell her about office drama and then says we should go out for drinks this week. I'm nervous to find out what will be thrown at me next."

"Mmm—you do work an awful lot. Maybe this will be good for you."

My gawking stare has her quickly adding, "Okay, fine, just be careful with that." Changing the subject, she continues, "So then we need to go shopping because you have to continue turning heads with your wardrobe. Oh, my God, you need some dresses for your trip. You know you're gonna have to dress up for that," she says and then smiles before finishing, "and… you can find some new shoes." Mabel wiggles her eyebrows, turns, and laughs as she walks to her room. "I'm going to change into something comfy and then let's hit the strip."

Shaking my head, I put my glass of water down and follow suit.

Wide waistband flare slacks along with a few barely boot cuts and a pair of ankle trousers or two. Yes, I like to wear pants. The blouses are where I go to create an outfit to be more my style. Flutter and bell sleeves, baroque tops among others, adorn the pants perfectly. I have plenty of jewelry to mix and match with these selections. I picked up four pairs of shoes even though I knew I didn't need them. Mabel laughed at me because I have shoes back at the apartment that will work beautifully, but I came up with some lame excuse. The only thing we didn't get was a couple dresses for the trip and that's fine. I can try to stumble over them this weekend.

We picked up Chinese food on our way back to the apartment. Both exhausted, I begin to wonder if Mabel didn't sleep well either. Since my arms are full of packages and carryout, Mabel has to open the doors and push the button for the elevator. Luckily, we don't have to wait long. My arms are screaming.

Oh, shit! Those ocean blues pull me into an undertow I can't swim out of—

He cuts his eyes away from mine. "Mabel." He nods to her before giving me his full attention. "Freckles." Fuck, if it doesn't sound like silk again. His lips turn up while he enjoys my speechless state at seeing him walk out of the elevator. He walks past me, and I swear, I leaned in to get a whiff of his cologne. *What is wrong with me?* Wait, *why* is he in my building?

"Gertie!" Mabel's shouts wake me up from whatever the hell that was. I quickly rush into the elevator stumbling. She pushes the button for our floor and eyes me hard. "You can't see him."

Cold.

Doused flame.

"What? I'm not seeing him, Mabel!" I retort.

She laughs. "Ha, yeah, that's not what I see this leading to." I scrunch my eyebrows in confusion. "Gertie, he is a big time player from what I hear with the girls."

"How do they know Mr. No Name?"

Mabel's eyebrows scrunch. "Mr. No Name? His name's Adam and everyone knows that douchebag, Gertie." The elevator dings and we proceed to our apartment.

Walking into my room, I realize a date with my little friend might get Mr. No Name, or shall I say, Adam out of my system. I make quick work hanging up my clothes, tucking away my shoes so that I can grab a plate and settle in front of my laptop. So what if he's a player. I never had any intentions of seeing him again. *Liar.* Shut it, Gertie!

Great, now I'm talking to myself, too. Firing up my laptop, I check my emails and find something from Rachel. Dear Lord, leave me alone.

From: Rachel Dumascus
Date: Monday, 3 March 2014 7:20 P.M.
To: Gertie Sawyer
Subject: Hey girl!

Let's grab a drink after work tomorrow. We'll discuss our upcoming trip.

Regards,

Rachel Dumascus
Head Editor-in-Chief
Simple Luxury
Houston, TX

My shoulders slump in defeat. I don't want to go out for a drink when I need to work on a couple of projects and not waste my time lollygagging like Mabel does with her friends. How do I respond to that message? Let me sit on it and think. If I respond, then she's going to expect me to answer her emails when I'm home. *Right?* Unlike her, I *do* know where to draw that line. If I don't respond, she might think I don't take my job seriously. *Shit, shit, shit!* I'm going to reply now. *Dammit!* After a quick reply of 'that sounds great', I hit send and move on to others and then to a little research.

Mabel's step halts my fingers running feverishly across the keyboard. "You're still at it?" she asks surprised.

"Yeah, just finishing up this one thought and then I'm going to call it a night."

"Don't forget you need to call Rick." She smirks and then sticks her tongue out at me.

"Yeah, yeah, yeah." I sing. "I know. I'll call when I get in bed."

"Aw, are you going to have Mr. Latin Lover put you to bed?" She giggles.

"Kiss it," I quip. Rick is like a brother to me. He's been there the last three years, literally helping me and picking my shit up since douche bag supposedly got drunk and slept with the town tramp. I love Rick. Gram, Mabel, and I are his family. Oh, he has parents, siblings, you know, the whole shebang, in Dallas. Trouble is they don't accept him. So, he said 'Fuck all y'all,' in so many words, and now he lives with Gram. This, frankly, is a blessing because I haven't been able to bring myself to go back since the day he came across one sprawled out Gertie on Tyler's front lawn.

"You better call. He's not happy with you." Mabel fidgets with her fingers. "I know it's my fault you were upset last night, and I promise to never do that to you again, but you mean so much to Rick and me."

"Thanks for the guilt trip, Mabel." I finish closing my laptop and head toward my room to complete my nightly routine so I can make everyone happy and get the phone call over. The problem is that Rick always makes me feel guilty.

Thirty minutes later, the line is ringing. Second ring, and then, "Well, well, well. If it isn't my gorgeous Gertie." I smile at his usual salutation.

"What up, dude," I quickly retort knowing how much he can't stand it when I call him dude.

"That hurts, darling." I chuckle at his antic. "Are you okay?" His voice turns sincere. "Mabel's been hounding the shit out of me to get ahold of you. Kind of like a little Chihuahua nipping at your pant leg."

"You've been around Gram for too long," I joke. Silence fills the line and this is Rick's way of telling me to be serious. Rolling my eyes because he can't see me, I continue, "Yeah, it's all good."

"Bullshit, and don't you taunt me by rolling your eyes, bitch!" He raises his sassy voice.

"If you want me to be honest—"

"Always."

"It fucking sucks. I miss him so much it physically hurts sometimes. This evening I was telling Mabel that I miss his friendship. He had been there for… everything."

"Like your parents."

Sniffling, I whisper, "Yes."

"Gert, I know things didn't work out for you guys to keep your relationship at that level, but he does love you. He misses you just as much as you miss him." I try to say something, but he interrupts me. "Stop lying to yourself. Can you just think of the possibility you two weren't meant to be more than friends at the time, but that Venus and Mars had to get involved along with your hormones and you two explored something that shouldn't have happened in the first place—at least not then?

"I've sat back and watched you lose three years of a life you cherished. A life you have made me part of, Gert. I know how much you treasure people because you know how quickly life can be taken from someone. There is no going back and apologizing for misunderstandings, misconceptions, or deception. What you have is on the table right now, and darling, he was young, dumb, and full of cum." I gasp. "Oh, shut it. Now, back to the subject at hand—is that enough of an excuse? No. But, Gert, you need to move on and you can't do that if you continue to hide from what happened. It hurts you, Mabel, and Gram, and regardless if you care, it hurts Tyler, too. Hell, it hurts my fine ass even." This earns a chuckle and a heavy sigh.

Using my free hand, I wipe the sloppy tears and reach for a tissue to blow my nose.

"For the love of God, you have to blow that horn in my ear?" He barks on the other end.

"Shut up." I lay back, stare at the ceiling again just like last night, but for different reasons. Last night, I hated Tyler—or did I actually? Can I honestly hate the one person who made me laugh when my world was falling apart? Just because he did something stupid? Maybe Rick's right. Oh, God, he can never hear me say that. "Um…"

"Yes, Gert?" he questions. He is the only one who can call me that now. I even threatened Gram that I was going to have everyone call me Gertrude so that she'd call me Gertie. She was apparently very pissed when Mom and Dad named me. I've never minded my name. It's one of the few things I have left from my parents, so regardless of how quirky the name, I love it.

"I'll give it some thought," I respond and quickly add, "but I'm not making any promises."

"Fair enough. Just hear him out, please. I'm not asking for you to take his hand in marriage."

"What?" I squeal.

"Kidding! Ha, ha, ha. God, I love you, darling."

"Have I told you how much of a dick you are lately?"

"Aw, shucks, you warm my soul. Sweet dreams. I'll catch ya tomorrow."

"Love you."

"You, too." I place my phone on the nightstand after plugging in the charger and bring the sheets up around my neck.

Have I made a mistake by giving up on our friendship? Closing my eyes, I picture a little boy and girl jumping off the dock and into Lake Eufaula behind Gram's house and where we spent countless hours rocking on his Mom's porch swing. Tears escape my eyes, and I have a feeling I might need to spend extra time on my eyes again in the morning.

Thirteen

*"Humans need to learn to play fetch. It is through my
observation that their minds need the exercise."*

~ *Cujo*

Tyler

Pacing.

I've been pacing for the last two hours outside Gert's
apartment complex. I have managed to ride the elevator to
the second floor to only chicken out, descend back to
ground level, and walk outside. I wish I smoked. At least
then I'd have something to do other than wear out the
pavement.

My phone dings.

Rick: Where the fuck are you?

Me: Get your panties out of a wad. I'm outside.

Rick: It's almost midnight.

Me: No shit!

Rick: You better get your ass up there or I'm going to call Gram.

Oh, hell, no!

Shit, shit, shit. Gram will kick my ass for sure if I don't get Gert to listen. She and Ma scare the shit out of me when they get their heads together.

Me: Fine, asswipe!

Rick: Good girl.

Me: Fuck you

Rick: Anytime, darling.

Me: You make me uncomfortable.

Rick: Aw, are we having a moment? Smoochies.

I don't respond. There is no winning when it comes to Rick. That's another one I'm afraid of—he has loved Gert through all the heartache I caused and managed to persuade Mabel to let me back in her life and Gert's lives. I'm thankful she's had him and even happier that he bats for the other team. Otherwise, I'd be one jealous fool.

Now I have to wait for someone else to come in or leave thanks to the locked door. And here comes someone. *Yes!* He pulls out his key and, bam, I'm in.

Courage. I seriously could use a little more.

Thankfully, the guy didn't get on the elevator. I guess he went to check mail or something. Over the last few hours, I've gotten to know this place pretty well. Pushing the elevator up-arrow button, I fold my arms across my chest and try to wait patiently. Lucky for me I don't have to wait. The doors open and this is when my chest feels like it has a ton of bricks pressing down on it. With shaky hands, I press the button labeled with the number two and lean back against the wall. Closing my eyes, I try to gain some sort of steady rhythm to my heart. I need this to work and to be able to say the right thing.

All too soon, the doors open and my heart picks up extra beats. I step off the elevator and suddenly feel out of breath. I need to just get it over with. Reaching her door, I begin to pound my hand hoping she'll be the one to open it and not Mabel.

No answer.

I bang again and rest my head against her door. *Please, God.*

No answer.

I bang again refusing to leave. She's in there. I know it.

Gertie

A pounding sound stirs me. Looking over at the monster, I see it's already midnight. There's that pounding again. I sit up, rub my eyes, and throw the covers off before climbing out of the comfort of my bed. Who the hell is banging at this time of night? The pounding continues. Mabel is snoring and wouldn't be able to hear anything thanks to her god-awful sound machine. Most likely the reason she didn't hear yesterday morning's commotion. I can't stand the white noise that thing makes.

As tired as I am, I do something very stupid. I open the door without looking to see who it is.

Tyler.

"What are you—"

"Gert, we have to talk." He pushes himself inside closing the door behind him with his foot. Standing over me, breathing heavily, his nostrils flare with his chest moving up and down in a dominating manner. I can't move. His presence at the moment is too much. "I've missed you," he finally says after staring for so long.

My breath hitches. *Oh, Tyler.* I've missed you, too— but can I admit that?

My head lowers and I close my eyes trying to will away the tears. His finger reaches under my chin to lift it until our eyes lock. Letting go, he moves his calloused fingers to swipe a fallen piece of hair out of my face tucking it behind my ear.

"Gert," he whispers.

Closing his eyes, he leans in to rest his forehead on mine as his hands simultaneously run up and down my arms trying to soothe something we can't define. It causes me to close mine as well as I try to keep the threatening dam from breaking after one tear escapes me. "I know you hate me, but I miss you. I need you to hear me out." I pull back to look into his eyes. "Gert. Can I stay here tonight?" My eyes nearly pop out with his unexpected question. "Just snuggle. I need to hold my best friend and the girl who owns my heart, soul, and my entire life." I immediately wrap my arms around his neck not wanting to let go. What on earth am I doing? Last night I slapped him, and now I'm holding onto him for dear life.

Damn you, Rick and your unsolicited words! It's your fault.

"I've missed you, Tyler. So damn much." I admit while he holds me tight against his chest. "But I need to know something... Something that's been bothering me since..."

"I'll tell you anything, just please ask rather than shut me out." His soft breath tickles my face.

"Why..." I close my eyes for a second and sniffle. "Why her?" My eyes plead with his. "Of all people, why her?" Tears slip down my cheeks as I await his response. Our breaths bridge the gap of words too numerous to speak at the moment.

"Gertie, that night I will forever regret because it tore us apart. I have no idea what happened. I was at the bar drinking with the guys. I was so excited to see you in a couple of days and one drink led to another until I lost count. All I talked about was you. I remember that vividly until the night escaped my consciousness. I haven't touched that hard shit since."

"Did you drink shots?"

His head sinks in shame as the air leaves his lungs. "I'm so sorry for doing that, too. I know how much that changed your life. I'll never do it again. I promise."

I cry out, "It killed my parents, Tyler." My hands grab his arms shaking them. "Mabel and I were supposed be with them that night." Sobs become uncontrollable. "The drunk driver... he... he..." I can't finish."

"Come here." He pulls me tight into his chest. "I was a dumbass, Gert. I wish I could go back and change what I did."

I hesitate as I want to believe him—a young, stupid guy. But after three years, I'm not so sure.

"Tyler, I don't know what to think." Exhaustion has my head falling into his chest.

"Gert, please let me stay and hold you." His arms wrap me tight while my thoughts metastasize over infidelity, deceit, and loss—loss of time, memories, and love.

My hands push him back a little giving myself space to breathe my own air and try to find the successful woman I've become. "I don't know if that's a good idea. I need time. This is so much to process and I'm scared," I bellow. "My heart can't take another—" If I'm honest with myself, I might be exaggerating.

"Gertie, I'm not here expecting you to forgive me over night after all this time. I just want to hold you. Please." He exhales heavily. "Please, just let me hold my best friend who I've longed for."

My guard obliterates and I find myself nodding into his chest. I might be the biggest fool right now for letting him in—knowing it's only a matter of time before he works his way into my damaged heart. I do know Tyler, though. It was only that one time when he hurt me. Yes, it broke me and forever changed us, but he's not a malicious person.

Walking around him, I secure the lock, grab his hand, and lead him to my bedroom. I'm tired of the constant battle with my heart. Tonight, I'll let go and be comforted by the best friend who was always there for me. He closes the bedroom door quietly and then his gaze locks on mine again as the moonlight highlighting his strong features. "Come on." He pulls me toward the bed letting go of my hand to remove his shirt and jeans. I slide into my treasured sheets with Tyler climbing in behind and snuggling just as we used to fall asleep many nights so long ago.

"I love you, Gert."

"I love you, too." I let go of my fake façade and tell him the God's honest truth. "But, we need to talk. There is so much—"

"Not tonight. Let's just get some sleep. I promise we'll talk. We may live in two separate towns, but I'm not going to allow time to slip away from us again." He kisses the side of my head and then settles on my pillow with me engulfed in his arms. Sleep rapidly sweeps me away with the comfort of home wrapped around me.

Tyler

She's so fucking beautiful. Starting with that mouth of hers—a mouth that I want to taste. I wonder if she tastes as good as she did years ago, but I can't. Not yet. I won't do that to her. She's going to need time, and I need her to know everything before…

I'm so scared.

What if she hates me after she finds out? Could I lose my Gert forever? At least I've held onto the possibility of a future over the years—could that possibility be gone after I show her?

Her beauty has me trying to control my dick that's so in tuned to her. After waiting a moment to calm the boy down, a question vomits its way out of my mouth.

What the heck was that, Tyler? Why would she allow me to stay? I'm such an idiot!

Her admission to missing me along with wrapping her arms around my neck brings thoughts of home, love, and a life together, all wrapped up in one. Damn, she fucking owns me.

Shit, get yourself together, Tyler! How can I, though? Our eyes catch the others and a million things are said but unheard. The only witness is the moon illuminating our conversation. A spotlight on moving forward, hopefully, in each other's lives. If only as a friend—it's not what I want, but my wants and needs are nothing compared to hers.

Thoughts too much to bare, I reach to pull her toward the bed and into me. After removing my shirt and jeans and saying a few prayers, my nether region is behaving. I rest myself behind and wrap my arms around her.

"I love you," I tell her and her response sends my heart into overdrive—and makes my dick twitch. *Damn hormones.*

I mumble words allowing my lips a quick graze on the side of her head planting a kiss and squeezing her tight. She must've been exhausted because her breathing almost immediately evens out as sleep takes her away.

I am laying here unable to sleep. The warmth of her body has mine screaming full of life. My head is swarming with possibilities. She told me she loved me. That's a start, *right?* Hopefully, she'll agree to come home soon. The need to show her overwhelms me. I pull my hand away just enough to trace her arm trying to remember and memorize all in the same thought how soft and wonderful her skin feels under my fingertips.

What if? I close my eyes trying to will away hope that could crush me tomorrow. Hope that this won't be the last time I ever have her in my arms. There is so much we need to discuss. So much that she needs to know and may not want to hear.

My fingers continue to trace her delicately while memories flood my mind.

Senior year of high school was our year. We were a full on couple sneaking any chance we had to make out. As seniors, we were already on cloud nine. Add the adolescent mind and hormones, and we were fucking superheroes. Gert's long strawberry hair flew in the wind as we held hands walking toward the school just in time to arrive at Mr. Ketters math class. I remember glancing over and seeing my entire future flash before me. It was filled with Gert.

Only Gert.

I squeeze my eyes hoping I don't shed a tear or two for our loss.

That day will always be burned into my memory because Gert's smile was not only breathtaking, but her eyes shown bright and she looked as if not an ounce of weight lay on her shoulders. Losing her parents nearly destroyed her, and at that moment, it was the first time I had seen her full of life. It was the most beautiful thing to not only see but also experience.

Her smile had faded and she looked away somberly when I continued to take in the awe-inspiring moment which snapped me out of my trance. "You're so beautiful, Gert," I tell her causing her eyes to reach mine again and that smile, fucking bright smile, reappears, and it hopelessly seeks an available place in my heart to hold onto. Only, Gert already had every piece of my heart. It beats for her.

Sadly, flashes of Gert finding me in bed with another woman pass before my eyes next. I wanted to punch something. I was so fucking pissed at myself. Holy shit, this isn't fair! It wasn't fair what I did to her.

It wasn't fair what happened.

Period.

Three years.

Gone.

Too many nights we lost because of it. My throat tightens and all I want to do is cry for the Gert, who I deceived and for her stupid boyfriend who hadn't known what happened. All I want to do is hold onto right now and I can't. *Shit, I can't breathe.*

I have to tell her, but not now. I need to get her home first.

Fuck, I can't think straight. The urgency to wake her is too much. I need to get out of here and gather my thoughts.

Quietly, I slide away knowing the only thing to do now is leave. Just before walking out, I turn and make the mistake of looking at my sleeping beauty. Stepping back, my body leans against the wall and I slide to the floor. Knees bent, I rest my arms on top of them unable to take my eyes off her sleeping form. Should I wake her?

Fuck!

I lean my head back and look up at the ceiling. If there is a God, I beg him to hear me now. Please don't let this be it.

Please...

Fourteen

"Why can't I pee inside? The cat does. It's raining outside and Mr. Prissy Pants thinks I should go outside in that weather. My poor wet paws are getting dirty."

~ *Cujo*

Gertie

What on earth is happening with this weather? Did hell freeze over? Winter is done. March isn't supposed to be this cold. I pull my thin sweater closer while I pick up the pace hoping it will warm me for the long-ass walk. Why didn't I bother to check the weather forecast? Oh, I remember. I was busy contemplating why Tyler was gone when I woke up this morning. Did he realize it was wrong to stay over?

As soon as the shock of the icy air hits me leaving the building, I open my weather app. Houston's high today is forty degrees—that's almost twenty degrees colder than average. Now, you argue that I grew up in Eufaula so I should be accustomed to the cold. Yes, the temperature dips to artic levels of twenty or so degrees. Roll your eyes because that's fucking cold. But, Houston is south, I repeat south, so in my haste and rush this morning, I didn't bother to prepare. See what happens when I deal with shit outside of work? Although I *will* admit that the feel of Tyler's arms around me was amazing.

Reaching the office couldn't come fast enough and I sag into the seat behind my desk. My feet ache from shopping yesterday, and every square inch of me is in a shiver spasm from that damn cold air.

"Morning," Penny sings walking into my office in an outfit that is best described as... bright. Whoever had designed the banana peel she's wearing needs to be incarcerated. I wonder if Jennifer has seen her. Bitch better not say anything to Penny. "Hello?"

Huh? "Oh, sorry." I shake my head trying to wake up.

"Damn, Gertie. You are out of it." Penny generously places a hot cup of coffee in front of me. Oh, bless her. Her kindness is overshadowed by the world wind also known as my personal life.

Grabbing the bridge of my nose, I close my eyes and try to kill the growing headache. I can't allow my personal life to interfere with work. I've got to get a handle on all the shit that's gone down in the last three days. That dream is all to blame. Taking a deep breath I respond, "I know, Penny, I know."

"Well, I think I better give you fair warning that Rachel is on her way over here—"

"Did someone call my name?" Rachel sings and smiles knowingly with a hand resting on my doorway and another on her hip. "Thank you, Penny. I'll take it from here." Penny rolls her eyes as she stands with her back to Rachel, and with a half-hearted smile that screams fake, she pivots and goes back to her station outside my office.

Rachel walks slowly toward my desk as if in a runway style fashion and makes herself at home in one of my leather chairs. "So, since Penny didn't have a chance to warn you," she drawls out 'warn' as if she enjoys making me squirm. "I get the privilege to tell you about an exciting trip we must take."

"Oh, will this trip be while we're in DC?" I ask focusing on firing up my laptop and shuffling files around. I can focus on two things at once and what she wants to talk about doesn't need a whole lot of brainpower. *I hope.*

"Well, no, not exactly. Simple Luxury is hosting a cocktail party Tuesday evening and I need to do quality control. This is your moment to shine." *Shine?* "As editor-in-chief, I oversee all aspects of publications in this office. We both know Alan didn't create the results needed to keep this office above its competition, so now it's my job to not only fix his mistakes, but to move our division of Simple Luxury in the direction of the vision of corporate." The way she speaks of my prior boss is making me uncomfortable, *again.* I understand he wasn't doing his job, but for heaven's sake, stop throwing it out there.

When I realize that she had quit talking but still lingered, I looked up. "As an editor yourself, Gertie, you understand the importance of staying focused on the overall vision. So, in an effort to put this division back on track, we need to pay the venue a visit ahead of time. Our lead photographer will be traveling with us along with Ms. Wells, who will be drawing up a story on the event and the DAR Headquarters picturesque venue."

I almost spit coffee on my boss and sit taller in my chair. *Shit*, Jennifer's traveling with us? I don't want to listen to her needless babble. "Uh... so when is this trip?" I ask as I mentally cringe at the answer she's about to give me.

Smiling, she answers, "Tomorrow." Rachel stands demanding my attention. "You'll need to be at the airport at eight in the morning. The company jet will be fueled and ready." She turns and walks toward the doorway she had just walked through moments ago, but turns around just short of it as she had done in the conference room. Must be some sort of signature move of *hers*. "Oh, have a great day Gertie and don't forget drinks. She smiles and leaves. I roll my eyes.

Tomorrow? Is that even within the boundaries of acceptable notice?

"Sorry, Gertie. I tried to get to you first." Penny rushes in apologizing like her telling me first would do anything to change my mood.

"It's fine, Penny." I throw my head down onto my folded arms that are now resting flat on my desk. I'm already counting down the time until I can walk out of this office and go home. I so do not want to deal with this. *Shit, drinks.* Ugh, I still need to figure out my mixed and raw emotions for Tyler. Dammit, here I go thinking about my personal life during work hours again. Shaking my head, I will away the urgency to internalize Tyler's actions. I'll hash out those thoughts on my walk home.

I decide it's best to begin unloading my backpack, opening browsers on my laptop, spray my perfume, and sip some more coffee. This day's gonna be better from this point on.

Ding.

What the hell? Seventy-two messages? I was just on here. Here goes nothing. Clicking the most recent message:

From: Rachel Dumascus
Date: Tuesday, 4 March 2014 8:03 A.M.
To: Gertie Sawyer, Jennifer Wells
Subject: Let's get on the same page.

Jennifer, I will need you to go directly to Gertie for any information regarding DAR. She is a registered Daughter and has a wealth of knowledge. Secondly, Gertie will be editing your piece on the event.

Gertie, we have a meeting with the staff at DAR Headquarters tomorrow evening. This will afford us the opportunity to go over details and make sure everything is in place. Pay attention because you are going to be my second-hand woman.

That is all for now. We'll go over more details on the flight.

Regards,

Rachel Dumascus

Head Editor-in-Chief
Simple Luxury
Houston, TX

Pay attention? Shit, does she know I have a tendency to zone out? And Jennifer is going to be pissed because she's been with the company longer than I have and here I come in. *Fuck!*

This is nothing like I experienced at Williams, a prestigious magazine company where I got my start interning. The owner, Peter, was such a pleasure to work with. He begged me not to go out on my own, offering me a job on the spot for me to stay. But I don't like hand outs, and I wanted to prove to myself I could do this without help from others. *Now, I wonder if it was a mistake leaving in the first place.*

Scrolling through my other emails, I find they can wait. I need to submit the files I edited last night. With twenty minutes of my day wasted on uploading files, I can finally move onto the next project. Foremost, I need to make sure I have everything I'll need for the trip.

"Gertie, line one is for you," Penny announces. Completely lost in work, I answer without bothering to ask who it is.

"Gertie Sawyer."

"Hello, Ms. Sawyer. How are you doing today?" *That voice.* My heart begins to race wondering what this call is about.

"I'm sorry, will you please tell me with whom I'm speaking?" I rather beg. *So unprofessional, Gertie!*

"My dear, you don't need to know. I'm calling to check in and make sure you understand all arrangements have been confirmed for your trip to DC tomorrow." *WHAT??*

"Uh... um... Will I be meeting you on this trip?" I question nervously.

"Time's up, have a good day, Gertie." Click.

Click?

Fucking click!

Pushing the button on the speaker, I exclaim, "Penny, I need you in here."

"Yes?" she asks walking inside my office.

"Who the hell was that on the phone?" I ask demanding to know who this person thinks he is. She brings her hands together and looks down at them. I can already tell she isn't going to tell me. "Penny, I need to know."

Waterworks. *What the hell?* "I'm sorry. I'm just not feeling well. My sinuses are acting up and my right ear began hurting last night." *Seriously?*

"What does that have to do with who was on the phone?"

"I couldn't understand him when he gave me his name," she sheepishly admits diverting her eyes.

"Penny, that's not acceptable. I expect you to do your job. Please, take messages from everyone for the remainder of the day. No more phone calls. Okay?"

"Okay. I'm sorry, Gertie," she cries pushing a tissue up to her nose. *Gross!* Have I mentioned I'm sort of a germaphobe? Yeah. That's why Rick jokes about Cujo. I know where Cujo's tongue has been and the thought of him licking me? *Ack!*

"It's fine. I'll talk to you later." And with that, Penny leaves closing my office door. Jesus, why didn't I do a better job researching Penny's previous employment history? Oh, that's right. It wasn't a big deal when I was working under Alan. I was able to work quietly. Second day working with Rachel and my nerves are fucking shot. I think I might actually need to talk to Mabel tonight. Quickly pulling out my cell phone, I send Mabel a text asking if she's busy.

Ding.

My eyes immediately shoot up to my inbox. *Rachel.*

From: Rachel Dumascus
Date: Tuesday, 4 March 2014 9:47 A.M.
To: Gertie Sawyer
Subject: Tonight

My boyfriend will be joining us for drinks after work. I can't wait for you to meet him.

Regards,

Rachel Dumascus
Head Editor-in-Chief
Simple Luxury
Houston, TX

Fuckity, fuck, fuck! Where is the line between reasonable and unreasonable? Am I going to be able to have a life outside of work? *Oh, for heaven's sake.* I quickly text Mabel again, letting her know something's come up and that I'm going to be busy—*oh, and I'm leaving for DC tomorrow.*

Immediately, she replies.

Mabel: DC? That's next week!

Gertie: Yeah, I know. Rachel sprang this on me this morning. Says we need to make sure everything's in order.

Mabel: Sounds like she's trying to take over your life, Gert.

I mean, Gertie.

Gertie: LOL I know. After I texted you earlier, she sends me an email about meeting her boyfriend when we go out for drinks.

Mabel: Tell her no.

Gertie: How can I? That would make her think I'm not taking this job seriously.

Mabel: *rolls eyes* You're full of shit.

Gertie: Whatever!

Mabel: What is this about Tyler sleeping over last night?

Gertie: No comment

Mabel: TELL ME!

Gertie: NO

Mabel: Dammit, Gertie. I'm going to kick your rear-end next time I see you.

Gertie: Lucky for me, I will be gone and you won't have the opportunity.

Mabel: You're a snot!

Gertie: Love you, too. BYE

Mabel: Don't you dare say bye. I'm older. I get the last word.

Gertie: Powering off phone. Toodles

And I do power it off. Mabel is so going to give me a verbal lashing later. I chuckle wondering what could be going through her mind about Tyler coming over. Hell, I don't even know. I need her help to sift through what's going on in my head.

'Knock, knock' echoes in my office. "How about that—" Rachel pauses. "What's so funny?" She raises an eyebrow walking toward the chair. Please, don't sit down. Please, for the love of God. Of course, she sits down.

"Nothing. I was just thinking about something." I try to dismiss before she drills further.

"Care to share?" she pushes. *Pushy much?*

"Nah, it' nothing. Anyway, what can I help you with?"

"Oh, just wondering if you got my email and if you're excited to meet my boyfriend." She thrusts forward.

"Uh… I just saw your email and—"

"You're excited, aren't you?" *Huh?*

"I actually need to pack and get ready for the trip. There are a number of articles that I need to proof before sending them to publication."

She waves her hand in front of her. "Those can wait. You're ahead of schedule, and I have no doubt you'll get it all done. So, let's grab a drink and let loose. I found out you walk to work, so we'll take my car and I can drop you off at home later." My God, this lady *is* controlling!

"Uh… okay… I guess."

"We need to work on your communication skills." I look at her quizzically because I'm confused. "Your answers are short. That's all." Rachel shrugs, places her hands on each arm rest, and lifts herself to stand over me. Like usual, it seems. "I'll come get you after work. Be ready at five." She turns and walks out. My eyes remain on the doorway waiting for her to turn back around and say something else, only she doesn't. Nor does she close my door. Sagging into my seat, I wonder if this is really what I want in my life. It's only been two days working with her. I know realistically, I have to give it some time. If things don't change, I'm looking for a new job, though.

Knuckles hit my door twice. "Are we ready?" How can five o'clock conveniently roll around when I'm up to my elbows in a story? "Tsk, tsk." She points at my desk.

"Give me a sec. I just need to gather my stuff." I quickly shuffle shit around my desk nervously and jam it all in my backpack. Guess I won't need to change into my tennis shoes this evening since she's all but demanded to drive me. I decide to leave them behind so that there's less to carry. After all, I am catching a flight in the morning. I'll deal with tennis shoes or lack thereof when I return.

Rachel claps her hands excitedly. "Let's go. I so need a drink after the kind of day I've had." *Really? She* needs a drink? Does she even work? Mentally putting those thoughts away, I toss my backpack over my shoulder and follow her.

Chaps. She chooses fucking Chaps as our go-to place for drinks. At least it's Tuesday and the crowd won't be wild.

Seated in a booth and drinks ordered, we begin to talk about stupid stuff like the weather and then she throws in an irritating subject. "I feel awful for Jennifer. She has her two boys both in wheelchairs to raise and has to work all day on top of it. I wish there was something I could do to help her." Internally, I roll my eyes.

Hold your tongue, Gertie. *Hold your tongue.* She'll figure out the lady has a bad case of Munchausen Syndrome and is a shit stirrer on her own one day—hopefully, sooner rather than later, so that I don't have to hear anymore.

I nod my head, not knowing what else to do. *Drinks arrive!* I wonder if she'll say something if I chug it. Oh, hell, who gives a shit? I take a large sip, gulp, or whatever—of my Cosmo. Yeah, I'm one of those who like to drink girlie drinks sometimes.

After pulling her domestic beer bottle away from her lips, she asks, "So tell me some good office gossip."

I shrug. "I'm not sure of any. I try to stay away from all the drama." Although Gram has called me a drama queen on numerous occasions.

"Oh, come on. You've got to have something," she pushes.

I take another sip, I mean, gulp. "Let me think," I respond as the waitress walks by asking if I'd like another. *Hell fucking yes!* "Okay, Larry in production had an affair with Elaine from the culinary writing department. Also, Nichole from the fashion department was fired for bullying one of the other members on her writing team. Those I remember Penny telling me."

"Oh… I think I need to hang out with Penny. She must have some good stories." Thank you, waitress, for delivering my next Cosmo just as I drain my first. I hand her my empty glass.

"Like I said, I try to stay away from all that. I think I have enough on my plate to worry about others—"

"Good evening, ladies. Freckles." He nods winking at me. *What the fuck?*

Fifteen

"Sometimes, I just close my eyes and dream that I finally catch that bugger."

~ *Cujo*

Tyler

When the hell will I get a wink of sleep? My head floods with thoughts of Gertie.

Her lips.

Her smile.

Her eyes.

Her stare.

Her faint breaths when she sleeps.

Her body.

Fuck, her body is amazing.

Beautiful doesn't even begin to describe what I see, what I feel, and what I want.

Tossing in the all too familiar hotel bed, I check the time. Eight-thirty-two in the morning. I wonder what she's doing right now. I'm sure she's at work.

My phone dings.

Rick: Call your mom. ASAP

Me: OMG, why? What is it?

Rick: Just, please call.

With my heart plummeting into the acid of my stomach, I immediately dial Ma's number scared something has happened.

"Tyler?" she answers deeply, clearly exhausted.

"What's wrong?"

Ma sighs profoundly. "It's okay... now, Sweetheart."

"How is she?"

"She's okay. It was just a fever. The doctor gave her a new antibiotic and sent us home," she finishes and all I can do is throw my head down while I squint back the tears. "Tyler..." I take a deep breath building courage to talk. "Tyler, she's okay, honey."

Heaving another sigh, I ask, "Are you sure? Did they do a full panel? Were her counts low? What was her blood pressure?" I begin reciting question after question usually directed to doctors.

"Sweetheart, stop. I've got this. She's asleep or I would give her the phone. Just do what you need to do so that you can come home to her."

"I'll be home tomorrow. Please take care of her." I finish the call and collapse every cell onto the mattress. Not now, God. Please, not now. I just lost dad. Why does life want to fuck me over? I need to see Gert one more time and get home. Determined to finish what I started when I came here, I move onto work. Knowing that things are not settled, but at least under control at this moment at home, will allow me the opportunity to focus on work and Gert. Ma will call me if anything changes.

Lunch comes and goes without a calorie intake. I finally shut my laptop around four in the afternoon knowing I need to eat and track down Gertie.

Damn if my heart isn't pulling in two different directions.

Sixteen

*"I've heard pure-bred dogs have some serious issues.
Thankfully, God made me a mutt. Humans are in no way pure.
They need to stop thinking that they're better than everyone else.
Hello? Everyone's poop stinks!"*

~ *Cujo*

Gertie

"What are you doing here?" I ask in utter shock and annoyance.

"Oh, you've already met my boyfriend?" Rachel responds cheerfully.

Goose bumps rise everywhere. He used me to cheat on my boss? Oh, my God. Oh, my God. What in the hell is *wrong* with him? "Um…"

"Gertie, we definitely need to work on your speaking skills. I hope that's not how you're going to talk while in DC."

"Huh? No. It's just…"

"What I believe Gertie means to say is that we've met." Ass-wipe chimes in. At that instant, I decide gulping my drink is what's best. Our overly attentive waitress, Becky, asks if I'd like another. My response, "Yes, please." Adam lifts an eyebrow and I quickly look away. Mabel warned me that he was a player. Oh, dear, my head is swimming.

"Oh, I see," Rachel retorts.

After draining my drink in a very unladylike manner, "Yes, you could say that." Thankfully, Becky returns. She's going to get a hefty tip from my ass. I wonder if she can read the thoughts going through my head. I begin to take a sip.

"Have you fucked my boyfriend?" I choke violently bathing Rachel with my drink from her question.

"Oh, no. I'm so sorry Rachel!" More than you know, I'm sorry for not only decorating you in Cosmo, but making out with your boyfriend, too.

"I take it that's a... yes?" She tilts her head to the side studying my reaction.

"No!" I shout appalled while my hands shake nervously.

She shrugs nonchalantly. "That surprises me." Her eyes travel up and down the parts of my body she can see above the booth. *As if!*

"Rach, she wouldn't," Adam admits.

Looking between the two, I ask, "Am I missing something?" Completely confused and annoyed that either would be discussing this, much less my sex life. "I'm sorry, but it's late." I begin to stand, but Rachel's relaxed disposition surprises me into sinking back into the booth, jaw open, catching flies, and wondering what is wrong with her.

"Gertie, it's okay."

"What's okay?" I ask in confusion.

"If you want to fuck my boyfriend. We have an open relationship. We don't keep secrets, and best of all, we share," Rachel explains causing my eyes to bug out. Becky hands over another drink and this time, I don't hesitate gulping the shit.

"Umm... I... uh... I'm sorry... if I, uh... gave you the wrong impression, but... umm... I don't do that stuff or relationships. I... uh... I... gotta go!" Tossing some cash on the table I stand noticing my vision is a little blurry and leave on wobbly legs. The dark, cold air strikes me just after waving bye to Sam.

It's then I realize...

FUCK!

My bag is in her car. Stomping my foot in an effort to relieve the frustration, I gather my remaining self-respect and walk back inside passing an amused Sam. "Something I can do for you, Gertie?" he asks inquisitively. I narrow my eyes at Sam's teasing tone, grab the end of my blouse readjusting it as I square my shoulders, and then proceed back to hell. Thankfully, Adam and Rachel weren't sitting by the window to witness my temper tantrum. Holding my head high, I approach the booth.

Adam spots me first whose lips begin to turn up in a mischievous smirk while his eyebrow lifts in that unfair sexy manner. How dare he make my hormones flip-flop. He and Rachel's relationship is insane.

"Can I help you, Freckles?" *Argh!*

"Don't call me that. It's not my name! This thing," my right hand circles between the two of them, "is demented. I'm not that type of person."

"Oh, come on, Freckles. It will be fun. I promise. And if I'm not mistaken... it has been a while. Hasn't it?" Fucking bastard drags out *hasn't it* as if it's going to change my mind.

"You're a slut," I point to Adam and then turn my annoyed attention to Rachel. "Is your car unlocked? I left my bag."

Rachel smiles knowingly. *What the fuck is this?* My eyes cut to Adam deciphering what she's smiling about. "I'll take her," he says in that voice so smooth it's like milk chocolate. Shit, I need to get laid or at least eat some chocolate. But I'll be damned if it's going to be with present company.

Shaking my head, I step back away from the booth waving my hands dismissively and— "Oh, my God!! I'm so very sorry," I apologize to Becky, who's now on the floor wearing whoever's order she was carrying. Can this get any worse? The cool liquid seeps through my clothes causing quite the chill. *Shit!* Looking behind me, I'm covered with some of the order, too. *Nice.* "Becky, I can't apologize enough. I'll pay for the order and your dry cleaning," I say trying to make amends while helping her off that dirty-ass floor.

"Gertie, it's okay. You can just owe me a drink next time we go out. Okay?" Becky kindly responds. Thank heaven I know her.

I twist around and demand, "I want my bag and nothing... I repeat nothing else from either of you." I storm out pursing my lips at Sam while I pass him once more.

Standing on the sidewalk outside, the cold air sends shivers over my entire freaking body.

"Come on, Gertie, don't be mad," Rachel pleads walking toward me carrying my bag.

"Let's just please forget it."

"The plane leaves at eight sharp," she says, turning to walk back inside Chaps. Pausing, she turns her head and says, "I expect you there..." and with a hard stare, she continues, "and on time, Gertie." Then she walks through the door.

Bitch!

I gather my bag below my sleeve while I speed walk toward my building and blindly search for my headphones. I need music. *How sick is that shit?* Happy with what my fingers find, I pull on the cord, sling the backpack over my shoulders, and escape in the music streaming through my headphones—only my thoughts go to Tyler.

It felt so right to have him wrap me in his arms. I thought he liked it too, so why did he leave? Confused thoughts play tug-of-war and the only way to shut everything up is to push the volume louder.

My focus should be on how I'm going to deal with Rachel tomorrow, not chasing a dream that died years ago.

The blood flowing within each vein warms as the adrenaline kicks into overdrive. Before I know it, I reach my building. Thankfully, because *holy shit* my feet ache. Thoughts consumed of Tyler, I barely remember the surroundings I had passed, or the fact that I was wearing the very heels I wore all day. But, damn if I don't sense it right now.

Once I get into the elevator, I pluck out of my heels and feel blessed when toes encounter the soft carpeted elevator floor.

The elevator stops and I begin to realize how sluggish my body is moving. Unlocking the door, I swing it closed and head straight for the shower to wash away the mess of food including all the annoying stuff from today.

Dressed in my normal pajamas—t-shirt and shorts, I quickly grab a couple of outfits, my suitcase, and toiletries, and then plop onto the sofa debating whether I have the energy to turn on the television. Yeah, not going to—

Mabel swings the door open standing before me suspiciously. I'm too mentally exhausted to question or describe the awful, bizarre night, much less the night before. I bet she's dying to know what's going on with Tyler. I think I'll second that. Shutting the door, she gets rid of her scarf and sweater, hanging them on the appropriate hook next to our rack of keys, before moving into the kitchen to open a bottle of wine.

"Is it a one or two glass night?" she asks. Raising an eyebrow, Mabel continues, "Better yet, is it an entire bottle kind of night?" I throw my head back not knowing how to answer, not sure alcohol can begin to scratch the surface of forgetting my day.

Suddenly, a knock sounds. My eyes immediately find Mabel's eyes. She raises her eyebrows, turns her lips downward into a frown, and shrugs to let me she doesn't know who it is. I can barely move from walking home in those heels. Why I have a thing for shoes with heels, I will always question after tonight.

Please don't be anyone with drama. I don't think I can handle anymore tonight.

Mabel answers and the voice that returns her hello has me rising to attention off the sofa. My body reacts as if we've been together this entire time.

Tyler.

Whatever is happening between us must be notified. "Umm... I think... I will... umm... check the mail." Mabel says, grabbing her keys and shutting the door. Tyler stands motionless much like I do.

"Sorry I left last night." His hands remain tucked away in the pockets of his jeans while he sheepishly looks down and then back up at me. He appears either embarrassed or uneasy—or maybe both. Handsomely standing in his worn jeans, sweatshirt and the... my eyes linger noticing the boots I remember helping him pick out years ago.

I cock my head to the side as tears blur my sight. Do I want to question why he left? Or do I just want to feel his touch, his lips, his... Before I give it a second thought, and in one swift move, I wrap myself completely around the man I love. His arms immediately cradle and support my weight as he buries his head in my neck.

Home.

"Sorry," he murmurs. I pull back to look into his deep blue eyes. It hits me hard.

"I need to know something, Tyler. I have so many questions, but most importantly, I need to know..." The knot in my throat causes me to stop. He can sense my voice is full of sadness.

"What is it?" he asks pulling me over to the sofa. My legs settle on the sides of his body.

I take a deep breath before beginning. "The last three years have been awful." Tears sting my eyes and it's no use. I start sobbing. His arms tighten with one hand rubbing my back trying to soothe the pain. "Have they been hard for you, too?" I stammer.

"I'm so sorry. I never meant for that to happen. Like I told you last night, Gertie, I was so excited about you coming home for spring break. I know it's not an excuse, but that night..." He pauses closing his eyes, and my heart almost breaks for him... for us. "Gertie, I have no recollection of anything. You have always been the only one I want and need. I love you and have spent every day the last few years trying to make things right." I pull back to look into his eyes. "One thing you need to know is I've known where you've been, but I realized you wouldn't—"

"What?" I cry cutting him off. "Why haven't you fought for me? Is she... I mean, are you two..."

"No, Gert. I haven't been with anyone since that night." He sighs. "I just didn't know how to get you back. You rejecting me had been my biggest fear. At first, Gram wouldn't tell me where you were. She gave me the cold shoulder until one day she showed up on my doorstep."

I lean my forehead against his and readjust my legs as they begin the first signs of falling asleep. "Gram never told me," I respond in confusion. *Why didn't Gram say something to me?*

"She said I needed to be punished."

We both chuckle lightly at Gram's old ways.

"But why didn't you come sooner?" I question with my fingers lightly running up and down his arms.

"The only way I ever had a chance with you was if I stayed and worked my ass off to help dad with the company. I want to be able to provide, and if I chased after you, Gert, there was no way my head would have been in the right place to do that." A tear seeps from his eyes. "I need to tell you..." He pulls me tight. "Dad passed away a couple of weeks ago, and I knew then I had to come. I couldn't let another moment slip by without you knowing how much I care. How much I still love you."

"Oh, Tyler." I sob. "Your dad?" We both cry and hold onto each other. "I'm so sorry, Tyler! How... what happened?"

We're both silent for a moment.

"He had a pulmonary embolism." He breathes heavily through his stifling tears. "Doctor's discovered it was caused by pancreatic cancer." Another pause. My throat is so tight from grief that I can't say anything. "It wasn't the cancer that killed him, though. He developed more clots. They rushed him into surgery, but he didn't make it."

I tighten my hold on him wanting to take some of the pain away, but also I grieve the loss of a man I grew up knowing as a second father. I loved him so. He and Mrs. Jackson were amazing people.

"Dad wanted to see you so bad. I was coming to get you and then he got worse. I couldn't leave. It was touch and go, and Mom needed me."

"Oh, your mom. I've missed them terribly."

"I know, Gertie. Mom and Dad never stopped loving you either." His admission has me sobbing harder. Why was I so foolish to throw away my life back home, throw away the very people who were always there for me? What the hell was I thinking?

We hold onto each other as I wish more than anything to rewind time.

"Gertie, I feel like I stole so much from us. Do you think you'll ever be able to forgive me?"

I pull back and gaze into his eyes for what feels like hours. It's easy to get lost in his deep blues, only now they've grown darker as if a storm was brewing.

"Tyler, I'm not going to pretend. I haven't been able to date or see anyone because I'm scared of being hurt again." My shoulders slump thinking of how long it's been since I've been with someone—not just anyone, Tyler. I lean my forehead on his chest unable to watch the hurt transform in his eyes.

"I swear to God, Gertie, I will live my entire life trying to make up for what I did." I nod and find my face in his neck holding onto this moment. His fingers run through my hair and I realize now mine are doing the same thing. "Hey," he pulls back, "can you take some time off work and come home?" My eyes lower while I think about whether I can handle going back to all those memories. But as he said, we don't know what tomorrow holds, so I better go now while I can still be with those I care about. I would love to see the woman who treated me as a daughter for so long and sadly pay respects to Mr. Jackson. My mind immediately goes to my parents. It's about time I visit them as well. "Gert, there is something I want to show you." Lifting my chin, he continues. "Could you let this be the first step in allowing me to earn your trust back?"

"Umm... I'll try," I whisper softly. Maybe nervously, too. Small town Eufaula will be all up in our business. "So, what is it that you want to show me?" I question playfully trying to lighten the mood. It's too much.

His laugh vibrates through his chest and I smile. "I can't tell you." When I draw my eyebrows in confusion, he adds, "It's something I need you to be there to see." His fingers trace the side of my face in an endearing fashion. Many won't be able to understand how easy it is for me to let go of the pain he caused. But Tyler and I have a history like none other. We have a bond that I now realize isn't easily forgotten, nor can it be thrown away. He's been hurting as much as I have. He wouldn't lie. That's not my Tyler.

"Fine," I blow, "but you remember how much I hate surprises." The pain on his face vanishes.

"Oh, yes, I remember," he says deviously as a sinister smile grows. My mind tries to calculate the number of days I have saved to take off and it's no use. Tyler pulls my head toward him just before his lips meet my cheek.

There is nothing left to be done.

It's over.

I don't want to fight this anymore. I just hope I can get past everything else and that my heart won't be broken again.

Without hesitation, I turn my head so that our lips crash taking over any other thoughts. His tongue runs along the crease requesting entrance. However, no permission was required. Willingly, I open. His taste is a drug, one I'll never get enough of. I push away my heartache and beg for his love to seek a way inside to heal and rebuild our hearts. My fingers thread his hair and a moan escapes me.

"Gert…" Tyler manages between kisses. I don't want to have a conversation right now. At least not with *words*.

"Make love to me," I plead. He immediately pulls back causing a shiver from his intense stare that is heavy with desire. Our mouths find each other's again. Without a second thought, his grip tightens and he stands to lead us to my room kicking the door closed once we're through it.

Gently, he lays me flat on the bed with his body following suit. Resting on one elbow, he hovers over with eyes searching my soul. His gaze drifts to the fingers he's using to gently brush the side of my face. Eyes remain on his fingers as they lower to my neck. My breath quickens with hunger. Seeing my reaction to his touch, he returns his eyes to my heavy lids. I'm battling to keep them open to make sure this isn't a dream, but the magnitude of feelings is too much.

Slowly, he lowers his head. It's painfully slow with his eyes dancing between my eyes and my lips. It induces me to lick the already plump lips from our kisses. His pupils darken following through with the descent. I wrap my legs around his waist welcoming the pressure he adds. My hands trace his, *holy shit*, his defined back. He looks and feels different from the last time I saw him. He's become a man. And damn does it feel good.

His fingers slide down to grip the edge of my shirt as he removes the flimsy fabric within seconds. Wild hands make sure his shirt is joining mine on the floor just as fast. With the space between us, he takes the opportunity to check out my breasts. A devilish grin grows as his hand reaches to squeeze them. "Damn, Gert," he moans. "I so fucking love your body." Instantaneously, I grow apprehensive of my appearance. Tyler notices the modification in my behavior. He wraps his arms around my back, pulling me onto his lap. Nervously, I place my arms around him and close my eyes to conceal my modesty.

I've always been self-conscious about my body. I hate to be so insecure, but I want him to love what he sees.

His hands cradle my face. "Gert," while his breath kisses my face, "Gert, open your eyes." I do as he says because there is no more hiding from him. "You are beautiful... and always have been. When I caught sight of you the other night, my heart nearly stopped. You hold it, Gert..." he pauses to kiss me again, "and you invariably always will... because it beats for you."

The tears sting my eyes again. "Oh, Ty. I've missed you, this, us..." I smother him with kisses that quickly become urgent. We both moan when I rock my hips. "I've never stopped loving you," I spill without a thought.

Shit. *Fuckity, fuck, fuck, fuck, fuck, fuck.* That was too easy to admit. He stops kissing me and leans his forehead against mine. "Gert..." he sighs heavily, "I'm so fucking sorry for what I did to you." His voice is laced with unfathomable pain.

I take a hand and run it along the side of his head, hoping it soothes some of the sorrow. It hurts to see him filled with so much regret and anger toward himself. "Ty..." I hesitate as I rest my head back on the pillow while I hope to find the right words. Taking a deep breath, I look him straight in the eye. The moon once again is witness to the words spoken and unspoken. "I love you." My eyes close as I continue. "I know you didn't mean to hurt me. It was three years ago and I still love you with all my heart. I don't know if I'm capable of not loving you. It certainly appears I don't know how because I know you feel this." I reach for his hand and place it over my heart. "You own this. I don't know what happens tomorrow, but I want and need tonight." I lift my gaze judging his reaction.

I gasp.

Tears.

Tears bleed from *both* of our eyes.

"I don't know what I did to get this second chance with you, but, damn woman, I never stopped loving you either." His arms hold me tight while we hold onto our love for one another. "There is so much more I need to tell you, Gert—"

I shake my head dismissively. "Not tonight... please." My arms squeeze him closer. "We both have regrets, but tonight, Ty, it's just you and me." I lift my lips to his ear and nibble. "Show me how much you love me... please," I beg.

His hand grabs a fistful of my hair, pulling it back so that our lips are once again where they belong. He tugs on my hair once more exposing my neck. Creating an exquisite trail along my sensitive skin with his mouth and tongue, he causes my senses to go into overdrive. "Only you," he whispers against my tender skin. For this reason, my body relaxes a bit more into his arms. "Only—"

"Gertie." *Shit!* "Gertie." Shouts from the hall echo throughout the apartment.

Tyler stops and lifts his head. When a smile tickles his lips, we laugh at Mabel's calls. "Should we say something?" I muse.

"Hmm… I don't want to let you go, babe," Tyler groans as he kisses me again.

"I don't want to either, but she's liable to walk in on us. I'll be quick." Reluctantly, I climb off his lap and the loss of contact is definitely mutually missed by our synchronized groans. I stumble searching for my t-shirt before opening the door to find Mabel beginning to knock.

"Oh… sorry… I… uh…" Mabel tries to form a coherent thought through her smile. Looking down as a blush heats my face, I turn around to find Tyler lying down with a smug grin. Damn, I need to get rid of Mabel. My body is calling for Tyler. "I'll leave you two alone. I was just checking on you." Mabel retreats slowly stepping back, clearly uncomfortable. Suddenly, her demeanor changes. "I'll be in my room if you kids need anything. Perhaps Rick will entertain me. She winks, turns, and doesn't look back.

Stunned at how well Mabel took Tyler lying in bed with me is confusing. I don't move as I try to process what the hell is going through her mind.

Soft music fills my bedroom and I turn around and close my door, proceeding with a smile toward the one thing that will either make or break me.

Tyler.

Need, desire, and want override any rational thoughts.

Standing before him craving the intimacy we once shared, I lift my shirt tossing it to the floor where it was earlier. No further movements are made until I decide to grip the waistband of my shorts and slip them down so that I'm only in my panties. If Tyler's animalistic growl is any indication of his self-control breaking, we're on the same page.

With a groan, he pulls me into him playfully and tosses me over on my back settling his body on top. "Fuck, Gert. I want to go slow, but I'm not sure if I can." He kisses me while I wrap my legs around him again.

"Please don't. I want you so bad." A lump forms in my throat when he squeezes my breasts working his way downward, placing one in his mouth, sucking and nipping the tip. Arching my back for more, he complies sucking harder before pulling it out and blowing on the tip. "Ty," I moan.

"What is it baby?"…kiss…"Do you like that?"…kiss. I respond with a breathless 'yes.' "I recall something else you like…" His lips run between my breasts and then further. Slow trajectory kisses are placed until he reaches my panty line. *Oh, shit!* The anticipation is becoming too much. His fingers hook the sides of my panties, sliding them down with his kisses following along the way. Once they're removed, his mouth and fingers tease their way upward. Instinctively, I spread my legs in an invitation. When his tongue hits that spot, my hips jump off the bed eliciting a chuckle from him where the vibrations of his laughter increase the riptide running through my body.

Shadows cloud my vision as he promptly sends me over the border into a blissful melody. "Damn, baby. I adore you," Tyler says kissing his way up to my breasts.

"Kiss me," I demand as I run my hand down his jeans, searching for the button to release the only barrier separating us from taking this to the next level. "Ty, I need you inside of me... Please," I beg arching my spine as an ache begins to work again. He aids me in removing his pants as quickly as possible. Once we've accomplished that task, he grabs my hands, placing them above my head as he's done so many times before.

"I love you, Gert. Only you, baby," he says removing a hand to help guide himself to my entrance. Before pushing forward, he rejoins his hands to mine lacing our fingers. He sucks my bottom lip, giving us this moment in time to burn to memory.

"I love you, Tyler. Only you can heal my heart," I admit as he pushes himself inside filling me with love and ecstasy. We breathe in each other's warm breath while working toward a rewarding rhythm. He squeezes my hands and I do the same. This magical moment is so much more than either of us realizes.

Our hearts glow from the miracle taking place. We cry out not giving two thoughts to anyone being able to hear as we both reach the point of no return.

"Oh, my God, Gert. Are you close, baby?"

"Yes, harder," I plead and thankfully, he obliges. "Tylerrrrrrr... argh..." I cry out.

A moan sounds from deep within his throat. "Holy shit, babe…" His body stills while our breaths continue to fill each other. He releases one of my hands to caress the side of my face. "I love you so much. I don't ever want to let you go."

Tears fill my eyes at the enormity of his declaration. "Please don't let me go. I love you, too." Our eyes glisten from the moonlight making promises I pray we can keep. I don't ever want this night to end. He lowers his mouth, placing a gentle, loving kiss sealing our words.

Moments later, he rolls onto his back, pulling my body with him, and, unfortunately, removing himself from my warmth. I drape an arm across his chest and savor the feel of his muscled body as I draw and outline the definitions.

Thank God, I never went off birth control!

Seventeen

"That moment when my human wakes up, and then goes to put his slippers on to only find one missing. That's when I enjoy lying on the couch, watching him tear apart the house to find it. Hide and seek is one of my favorite games. Too bad humans are so eager to seek—they hardly ever find."

~ *Cujo*

Tyler

Heaven.

If this is what heaven feels like, I'll be damned if I miss another Sunday mass.

Holding Gert in my arms is unbelievably magical as if God created them to fit only her. The patterns she's tracing on my stomach and chest is an added bonus. I turn toward her to breathe in her scent after placing a kiss on the side of her head. My hand slides under her chin lifting it to my lips.

"I have only ever loved you, Gertrude Ann Sawyer."

She slides her sexy ass body on top of mine. "Ty, I love you, too."

Hungry kisses take over and we find ourselves in the second round of showing each other how much we want to connect. I don't think I'll ever finish showing her. Each time we're together, I will make it my mission to help her heal. To help us move forward.

Oh, shit.

Gertie straddles my body and begins to move her hips. *Damn.* My hand instinctively searches for her sensitive spot to help her feel just as good as she's making me. "Mmm... Tyler..." She keeps making noises that are liable to make me come on the spot.

"Babe, if you keep making those... babe... shit!"

"Come on, Ty, go with me," she pants breathlessly.

Stars. Her rocking sends me into a galaxy far away where stars illuminate the darkness and all is peaceful—a world where we've never been apart.

She slows her pace finally collapsing on me. We try to catch our breaths, but our mouths refuse to separate.

As the night wears on, I tell her that I have to leave in the morning.

She replies, "I have to catch a plane first thing tomorrow."

Huh?

"Where are you going?"

"DC." She silences to a yawn. "There's a big convention next week. Simple Luxury…" she turns to look up, "the company I work for is hosting a cocktail mingle next Tuesday night, so I have to go tomorrow and make sure everything is in order."

"But you're an editor. Don't they have people who deal with that stuff?" I ask confused.

"We do. There are some other things I need to prepare since we're putting together a story on the event. It's kind of a big deal." She smiles.

"Sounds like you enjoy your work."

After a long sigh, she says, "Most days I do. I've always enjoyed reading and working with the authors, but this week has been bizarre and it's only Tuesday."

"How so?"

"Well, I met my new boss yesterday, and I get the impression she wants to be best friends already. And the guy you had the unfortunate opportunity to witness me with the other night is her boyfriend."

"Wait… what?" Thoughts bang around my head unable to follow.

"I was propositioned tonight." She laughs. "I don't think it's funny, but damn, I've never been asked something this crazy as I was asked tonight."

"Are you serious?" I ask rising on an elbow.

"What's wrong?" she asks.

"Please tell me you aren't thinking of going through with it," I beg.

She sits up pulling the covers over her chest. "I cannot believe you are asking me that question." She places her head in her hands and sniffs.

Oh, shit!

"Gert, I'm sorry. I panicked." Wrapping a protective arm around her, I lean into her hoping I can fix my stupidity.

She pushes me away and slides to the side of the bed. *Oh, fuck, NO!*

"Babe, please. I didn't mean it like that. I wasn't thinking. Come here, we just had some fucking amazing sex. Upsetting you was the last thing I meant to do."

"Tyler, that's it. We poured our hearts out for each other tonight and then you make a comment like that? I won't lie and tell you it didn't hurt. And for the record, no. I have no interest in anyone, but..." she pauses as more tears spill and her breath becomes troubled.

"Come here." I wrap my arms around her and allow for the years of pain to shed. "I'm such an asshole. I adore you, Gert, and if there is one thing I'm certain of is that I want a future with you in it."

She lifts her head. "I want that, too," she looks down, "but I'm scared. My world crumbled that morning, Tyler. I'm not sure if my heart can take that again."

"Sweetheart, I made a stupid mistake. But there are some things I need to say that might surprise you. Not only do I need to tell you, I want to tell you."

"I'm not sure my head can take more. Can we talk about it the next time we're together? It's late and we both have to get up early." She reaches up to lay a hand on the side of my face.

"So… you're going to DC tomorrow and next week?" I ask.

"Uh-huh." She leans in for a kiss and whispers, "I love you, Tyler. Please don't hurt me again."

Closing my eyes, I will away the painful tears. I lean in to kiss her nose. "I love you, too, baby." *I'll spend my life trying to make everything up to you.* I think, we're both asleep within minutes.

Eighteen

"I tell you what. If I smell a female's pee with those delicious pheromones, I'll certainly oblige and never miss an opportunity to mate. Food and sleep will sustain me until I get my groove on. Why must humans be so senseless to play a cat and mouse chase? I'll gladly get stuck with any female for those few minutes of howling fun."

~ *Cujo*

Gertie

The monster sounds, and I want to throw it across the room. Reaching to turn it off, I sense an empty bed. Where's Tyler?

I'm sore, so I'm pretty sure I didn't dream any of what happened last night. Shoot, I forgot to double check if I packed everything. Scrambling around, I throw in extra items and run for the shower.

Dressed, suitcase in hand, I walk into the kitchen checking my watch. Shit, seven. Take off is in an hour. I reach for my backpack and find a letter sitting next to it.

My one and only Gert,

I'm sorry I had to leave before I could tell you goodbye. Something came up and I have to get home as soon as possible. Please have a safe trip. I love you, baby, and can't wait to talk to you soon. Here's my number. Text me once you arrive in DC so that I know you're safe.

I love you, Gertrude Sawyer.

Ty

I smile, happy he didn't leave after regretting last night, and that it definitely wasn't a dream. Closing my eyes, I bring the note to my chest. Please, God... I don't know if I should pray that he doesn't break my heart or that we have a chance at forever because even if he breaks my heart, I'll have made more memories with him. That's the price I think I'm willing to pay if it means I have my lifelong best friend and boyfriend back in my life.

Tucking the letter in my backpack, I grab my bags and go down to the cab that's, hopefully, waiting. The driver appears irritated. Oh, I'm sorry I was... *what... one* minute late?

Settled in the backseat, I pull out Tyler's letter and my phone to program his number. Of course, I send him a message.

Me: I love you, Tyler Jackson

Tyler: Ah, you found my note. Good! I love you, too, babe. Sorry I had to run out early.

Me: Don't worry. Is everything okay?

Tyler: I think so. We'll talk soon. Gotta go, babe.

Hmm… so many questions begin to swim around. Strangely, he said he had something he needed to tell me. What does that mean? *Huh*…

I should text my Latin lover.

Me: Yo Bitch!

Rick: Aw, you're so sweet. Tell me. How's lover boy?

Me: I KNEW IT! Mabel told you, didn't she?

Rick: Maybe, baby.

Me: You're a dork!

Rick: I might have talked to someone else, too.

Me: WHAT??!!!! WHO?

Rick: Cujo says hi.

Me: You aren't going to tell me, are you?

Rick: Crap, I think Cujo needs to go for his morning walk. He stinks so bad that he left the room.

Me: You're an asshole.

Rick: Love you, baby girl!

Me: Kiss my ass.

I put my phone away. Ugh. If I didn't love him so much, I'd hijack Cujo and drop him off at Animal Control. A smile tickles me wondering what the look on Rick's face would look like. Before I can give it another thought, the taxi slows, and I find myself at the airport.

I pull up the email Rachel sent with the gate information. We're going on a private jet. This is all new to me. Walking through the terminal, I hear someone shout my name as they're running toward me. "Freckles!" I look up and bile immediately burns my throat.

Pursing my lips together, I tell myself I can do this. As if God tells me differently, I trip over my foot sending me into the arms of someone I have absolutely no respect for.

Adam.

"Thank you," I say through clenched teeth as I push myself up. Straightening my outfit, I begin, "Let me guess. You are going on the trip, too?" His smile is all the confirmation I need. *Nice.* I can do this.

I can.

I will.

Crap, I don't want to.

Ugh! Everything was fine until Rachel and Adam showed up and turned my world upside down a few days ago.

"Gertie, you made it," Rachel sings, eliciting an internal eye roll. My cell phone rings saving me from the fake broad.

It's Gram.

"Hi, Grammy."

"Darling, how are you?"

"Good. I'm getting ready to board a plane so I can't talk long."

"Oh? Where are you headed?"

"Um, yeah… about that... I may have forgotten to tell you something."

"Mmm… hmmm."

"You already know, don't you?" I shake my head. How she weasels her way into everyone's business is beyond me. Crap, she probably knows about Tyler.

"Perhaps."

"Okay, Gram. What do you want to know?" There is no sense in playing into her games. I just have to pull the bandage quick.

"Well, let's see. First of all, you better take lots of pictures while you're in DC. If you don't, I'll show up at the convention next week—and are you sure you'd like me there?"

"You wouldn't do that."

"Of course. I'm all for showing off my granddaughter."

"Please, don't. What else is there?"

She clears her throat. "It appears someone has had a visitor the last two evenings and failed to tell their poor, fragile grandmother, who constantly worries about her girls." I roll my eyes.

"You lay it on thick, don't you?" I ask exasperated.

"So, tell me. How is my Tyler?" *My Tyler?*

"Um…"

153

"Oh, don't you dare lie to me like you and Mabel do about going to Sunday mass!"

I gasp at her knowing too much about my life, but a smile immediately grows thinking about Tyler. "He's good, Gram."

"Are you back together?" *Are we? Oh, no, I don't know. What if we aren't? What if...* "Hellooo?" *Gram sings annoyingly as she interjects my one-sided mental conversation.* "Are you two back together yet?"

Yet? "I'm not sure."

"Give it time. The two of you will figure it out. He's a good man, Gertie. Please... oh, never mind." *What?*

"What are you not telling me?"

"Nothing, darling. Why would you ask such a thing?"

"Because it's you, Gram. What is it?"

"Darling, I can't divulge information like that."

"What information?" I ask irritated.

"Oh, dear. I need to go. I love you. Bye." She hangs up.

Seriously? What in the hell is going on and why wouldn't Gram tell me? She loves putting her nose in other people's business. What's keeping her from telling me?"

"Come on, Gertie, this way. We're taking off in five." I don't want to go on this trip. It's almost as if my heart is being pulled back to Eufaula, as crazy as that sounds. Tyler and I spend two nights together and look, I'm ready to fucking move my entire life for him. For us.

"Gertie and Jennifer, here is the itinerary for today and tomorrow. We'll be flying home on Friday." Rachel hands us each a folder that she could very easily have emailed. Thank God I'll be home for my Free Friday with the girls. I need to see what their thoughts are on all this crazy shit.

Nineteen

"Humans can predict what a dog is going to do next if they pulled their head out of their asses and just observed. Body language is sophisticated in mutts. Why do humans insist on ignoring what's directly in front of them? So many humans, not enough time to train them."

~ *Cujo*

Tyler

Damn, if I didn't get a text soon after falling asleep last night from Ma. Fucking had to stop for gas an hour outside of the metropolitan area. The station was closed at this God forsaken hour, but mercifully, the pumps were still working. Placing the nozzle, I walk away running my hands through my hair. I bend over wanting to cry. This shit can't be happening right now. I'm not ready.

Pulling on my hair, I look up to the sky and it's breathtaking as if God meant for me to be here at this very moment. I'm astounded. The number of stars is unspeakable and reminds me of the nights Gertie and I spent gazing at these very stars. Not a cloud in the sky to hide any of them. As I pray on each one of them, I feel a little bit more at peace. But dammit, I can't. There is so much unknown, unheard, and unfound that my mind continues to race. I need to get home as soon as possible. My heart tears in two separate directions. Letting out an exhausted scream for only the stars to witness, and possibly have my wishes come true, I head back to my truck. The nine-hour drive that took a little less than eight was painful with 'what ifs' swarming around my head. It's painful and fucking sucks.

The sun shines bright as I finally pull into the parking lot that I've become intimately familiar with over the last few months. I step out and stretch muscles I didn't realize I had until now. Pushing the button to lock my truck, I begin walking up the sidewalk that's been the centerpiece of my worry lately. I pull my sweatshirt tighter and cross my arms as I continue my journey.

Getting a call that late is never good, much less having to go anywhere in the middle of the night. That usually isn't favorable. I ride the elevator to the sixth floor. I'm sure I could take this route blindfolded and still wind up in the same chair I've sat in numerous times in the past month.

"Hi there, Mr. Jackson," says one of the ladies I've grown, unfortunately, to know recently.

"Hey, Janet."

"Go ahead, he's expecting you," she responds and I nod praying I'll be getting good news.

Slowly, I proceed turning the corner toward the doorway I hate entering.

"Tyler, thank you for coming." He reaches out a hand and I grasp it reminding myself that this guy is one of the experts. "Have a seat."

I uncomfortably take my normal position.

"I don't want to alarm you, but we found it has spread." When he finishes talking, I bend over and throw my head into my hands. "Listen. I can't imagine what you're going through, but the outcome is promising. While things were uncertain over the last twelve hours, I can tell you now that we've got a plan. That's why I needed to speak to you. I need you to sign some forms giving your permission." He stops.

Tears stinging my eyes, I raise my head to acknowledge his words. "You can get it?" I ask a little too hopeful.

"There are no guarantees, but I believe we can," he finishes and I almost round his desk to kiss his feet, but I can't get my hopes up. *Can I? How* much harder will this be if he can't?

No one told me how difficult this would be, but then again, who the fuck ever prepares themselves for shit like this? I close my eyes needing a moment to escape reality.

Gertie.

What would she do? And it hits me.

"Okay, where do I sign?"

A smile forms on his lips breaking the seriousness of the situation. I pray I'm doing the right thing.

I can't reciprocate the smile.

No.

I'm a mess.

Twenty

*"When will my cootie-freak human be back? Humans need to
take advice from dogs. Our ancestors, those who weren't
domesticated like me, had to suck it up and keep going.
Sometimes, I just want to sink my canines in her rear to snap her
out of it."*

~ *Cujo*

Gertie

The plane lands, finally. All I want to do is call Tyler. I'm
sick wondering what's going on. I can't shake this feeling
that something isn't right.

"Here. Let me grab your bag," Adam offers.

"No, thanks. I've got it." I pull my bag close to me
before exiting the plane. This is by far the last place I want
to be.

"Gertie," Rachel begins, "are you ready to see
Headquarters again? And if it's not too late, we can have
drinks afterward." Jennifer's eyes perk up and I just want to
roll mine.

Seriously? Why do I get the feeling she's pressuring me into *making* a decision that will benefit *her*? And that itinerary, yeah, that fucker says I'm sharing a room with Jennifer.

"Uh, yes, I am excited to see it again." I smile genuinely. "I'm pretty tired. Let's see how I feel after the meeting... I'll go as long as it pertains to business about the convention next week and nothing more." I want to high-five myself. Rarely do I stand up for myself like that. I must be getting my strength from Tyler. Please, God, let everything be okay and that we make it.

Since waking up this morning, I see Tyler everywhere begging for his mirage to be tangible. At every turn, a whiff of something familiar, the back of a head that could be a striking resemblance to his, or the way someone walks. He's all I see. Two nights and I've turned into a mushy love-sick teenager who can't stay focused on work. Then again, I've always had problems tuning people out all too easily.

I can't help it. Some people just aren't worth filling my brain cavity with an ounce of their gibberish. No one can fault me there. I deal with enough shit. Jeez, I already miss him. Miss what we were and can't wait to see what we can be. Damn, if I didn't have to work, I might be saying fuck you to Jennifer, Rachel, and her pet toy right now.

"Of course," Rachel responds and I sigh happily. We proceed to a waiting car, or shall I say, limo. Should I have expected anything different?

The ride is quiet while I play a bubble game on my phone. My concentration has diminished with hope and fear all wrapped in a sweet package adorning deep blue eyes and blond hair. I need to get it together.

Once in the room, I send Tyler and Mabel a quick text that I've arrived and all is good. I make quick work of hanging my clothes while Jennifer tries to tell me all about her son's recent problems. I don't mind listening, but it's all she talks about. Does she find some sort of sick enjoyment out of her son's disabilities?

DC is gorgeous and I truly want the opportunity to explore it. *Wow!* I've never been excited to do something like that in the last three years. Stunned, I stand still taking a moment to marvel in my new interests. Silently, I thank God and Tyler—and anyone else who may have taken part in all this madness.

My hotel phone rings. "Hello?"

"Meet us in the lobby in ten," Adam says on the other end.

"Okay." I hang up not wanting to give him the impression I'd like to stay on the phone a moment longer. Wait… that voice. Now that I think about it, his voice sounds just like the one who called my office twice asking about Rachel's accommodations and the trip. *What the fuck?* Why would he call me if… *NO!* Oh, dear God, please do not let him be employed with Simple Luxury, too. He can't. *Can he?*

If they're involved, it's a conflict of interest. *Shit!* I need to find out and quick because this can affect my job.

The elevator opens and the two of them sit cozy on one of the lavish sofas. Adam has his arm around Rachel's back. They look like a couple. *Hmm...*

"Oh, good, you're here," Rachel announces looking over her shoulder. "The car's waiting to take us to meet the staff."

Nervously, I follow Rachel and Adam outside into the chilly air. Jennifer sighs numerous times behind me as if something's wrong. Why does she always seem to be consumed with negativity and drama? I do my best to ignore her attitude and concentrate on getting through this trip.

The drive isn't far and the Memorial Continental Hall building is just as I remember. Large columns hold up the half-circular stately entrance. My eyes take in the intricate work and I quickly lose myself in the historical beauty once we step inside. Words escape me with each step. The foyer is magnificent. My Lord, I could spend hours studying the elegant architecture. My moment is lost when Rachel's booming voice distracts me.

"Gertie, right this way," she says as I grumble and sneak an extended gaze at the chandeliers. *Jeez...* That's a lot of glass. I wouldn't want to be the one in charge of cleaning all that crystal.

The staff, also known as docents and which happens to be all women, is wonderful and everything seems to be in order. Rachel sends Jennifer and me on a tour with a genealogist docent who knows the buildings inside and out along with the historical artifacts and life during that time period.

"Hey, so what direction do you want the story Rachel has me writing to go?" Jennifer whispers to me as she nudges me to keep up with the docent. *Excuse me?*

"Uh, Jennifer. This is your article, I'm only helping if you have questions and editing. I would advise you to take notes of the atmosphere, what you see, and facts the docent mentions. This is about the MEW conference and Simple Luxury. Although the time was anything, but simple, the values of home, God, and country was what was and still is the most important thing to preservation. Did you know that is the Daughters of the American Revolutions motto?"

"Oh… No, I didn't."

"You might want to do a little research."

"So you aren't helping me write it then?"

I stare blinking periodically at her ignorance. "No, I'm not writing the story with you."

She cocks her head in an annoyed fashion as if she's better than I am. *Whatever.*

"Fine," she finishes and my attention returns to the breathtaking details of each room.

Thank heavens for Gram's education and push to get us involved in our family heritage. Otherwise, I wouldn't understand how amazing this place is. I guess I would be like Jennifer. *Clueless.*

Then again… *Bad, Gertie!* Be nice.

After an hour and a half, we're on our way back to the hotel.

"We're just going to grab some drinks in the bar here," Rachel announces once the car stops in front of the hotel. I nod and follow the two with Jennifer quickly on my heels.

Uncomfortable much, Gertie?

Adam orders drinks. I would have protested, but it's something I actually like. Hopefully, I won't decorate Rachel with this one. "We need to celebrate this amazing opportunity. Not many get the chance to host an event at these conventions. We need to be on top of our game and keep things simple enough that we're not running around with our heads cut off," he finishes.

"Wait, Adam works for Simple Luxury?" I direct my question to Rachel wearily.

"Yes, Gertie, he does," she answers pointedly.

My heart beats faster in shock. Shit, I need to tuck this away and process it later. I'll definitely call Gram and get her take on it.

Turning back to the conversation, I ask, "Okay, but aren't there people we could hire to take care of things like this?"

"Gertie, the company is already forking over a lot of money. I assured them we could handle it, and I have every bit of confidence that we can perform," Rachel admits.

"So, what exactly are your expectations of me during the event?" I ask wanting it in black and white because the itinerary she handed me on the plane is vague, and I don't do vague.

"Very good, Gertie. As the itinerary states, we'll be making a full walk through with the staff tomorrow even though you had a chance to explore tonight with one of the docents. The staff will take care of the guests and any of their needs. What I would like you to do is take mental notes during the event and follow up on Jennifer's story. I want you to have fun next week, but please, keep in mind Tuesday evening Simple Luxury is on display. We cannot have any mishaps." I nod understanding my role.

Drinks arrive and I welcome the warmth it spreads throughout my body, taking some of the edge off.

"So... you want me to write the story and Gertie to edit it?" Jennifer repeats what has been told to her for the third time, but she says it with clear annoyance in her tone. My phone dings with a text message distracting me.

Penny: Gertie?

Me: Yeah, what's up?

Penny: I had no idea you worked at Williams. I hear you have to know the right people in order to even get a job cleaning toilets.

My heart pounds suddenly.

Me: What? How did you find out?

What the hell is going on?

Penny: Rachel asked for your resume.

Me: Why?

If this doesn't scream a high flying red flag, I don't know what does. Why does Rachel want my resume? I work hard and everyone knows that. Is she questioning my job?

Penny: She said something about a recognition speech.

Hmm...

I sit back in my chair and listen half-heartedly to the chatter amongst the table. Should I approach Rachel? Speaking of the devil, she keeps eyeing me. I wonder if her and Penny are chatting away, too since her phone is in her hands. I hate being acknowledged. It puts me back into the mindset of being in a small town with all eyes on me.

And when my mind goes there, it doesn't take long to remember why I left Eufaula. *Oh, no!* Can I forgive Tyler? Tears begin to cloud my vision, and I excuse myself to use the ladies' room.

Quickly pushing myself through the doors, I stop in front of the sink that hosts a large mirror. By this time, tears are streaming down my cheeks.

Three years of questions, wondering what he was doing, if he was hurting as much as I was, and missing those I turned my back on when I left flood my mind. I hate this. I lost the chance to create more memories with the Jackson family. Regardless if Tyler and I made it through his infidelity, they were still my second family. I dropped them and everyone except for Gram and Rick. What kind of person does that make me?

I collapse my elbows on the counter and case my head in my hands, sobbing years of anger and pain—along with the stupid girl who threw everything away while I thought Tyler was the one who destroyed my future. *I am so foolish!*

I need to go home, but more importantly, I need to call Gram. A quick text to Rachel will get me out of returning to the bar.

Me: Something isn't agreeing with me, I'm going to head back to the room.

Rachel: OK, feel better.

Rushing outside to find a private area, I dial Gram. "Hello?" she asks while I sink to the ground, thankful for the slightly warmer temperatures.

"Hi, Gram."

"What's wrong, darling?"

"I messed up big time."

"How so?"

"Gram, I don't know where to begin." Sobs overtake my voice.

"I see." She pauses while I just let the storm of emotions take over. "Darling, you want to be with Tyler, don't you?"

With a heavy breath, "Yes."

"Thank you, Jesus!" she exclaims.

I pull the phone back and look at it. Why I'm not sure, but it sobers my sadness. "Gram, what have you done?" I ask, knowing her all too well.

"Ohhh… nothing," she sings.

"I hope you are enjoying how amazingly foolish I feel right now."

"Of course, I'm not. But I will tell you this. It's about damn time you got your head out of your ass and realized what you've run from." My cries become louder. "I hope you know it's not too late."

I wipe my nose like a twelve-year-old. *Gross!* I brush my hand on my sweater wishing I had a tissue. Ugh.

"I heard about Mr. Jackson."

"I know. It's awfully sad, isn't it?"

"I never even told them good-bye before I went back to college," I admit.

"Maybe it's time you fix this."

I roll my eyes at Gram's words. "Gram, did you send Tyler?"

"Mmmm… I believe Tyler showed up on your doorstep, so how would I have sent him?"

"What are you up to, Gram?"

A little girl's voice sounds in the background. "Who's at your house?"

"Oh, it's a precious little girl I'm watching for someone."

"Huh." I sit straighter. "Tyler asked me to come home. He said he had something to show me."

"Did he, now," she responds, but not as a question.

"Gram!"

"What?"

"You know!"

"Says who?"

"Ugh, I can't stand it when you get like this."

"Oh, darling, I love you, too. So, tell me. Are you excited for Rick's visit this weekend?"

I chuckle thinking about Rick and Lord knows what we're going to get into. "Yes, but I want to come home. I need to see you and Mrs. Jackson."

"I know you do. It's time for you to set aside your pride and deal with everything that you've been running from."

I sigh. "Yeah, I'll see what my schedule is like in a few weeks. Gram?"

"Yes, darling?"

"I still love Tyler. I never stopped."

"Oh, honey, we all knew that already."

"We who?"

"Uh…" There is a crash in the background. "Oh, dear, I need to go, sweetheart. I'll talk to you soon. And, Gertie, I am very proud of you!"

After hanging up, I sit and ponder over my life and what's important. I love my job. Well, I did. Hopefully, Rachel will calm her tits and leave me be. I can't continue to work like this. Her demands and last minute shit is not how I work. Then, there's Tyler. Can we even have a future with his construction business in Eufaula and my job in Houston? I lean my head onto my arms that are resting on my knees. Would I be in the position I am if I hadn't run away?

My phone buzzes.

Tyler: Hey, babe. I miss you!

Wow, does he have ESP?

Me: I miss you, too.

Tyler: How's your trip going so far?

Me: Back at the hotel and Memorial Hall was just as gorgeous as I remember.

Tyler: That's awesome.

Me: Yeah, but something is weird. Rachel asked my secretary for my resume for some acknowledgement and I have no idea what for.

Tyler: Probably because you're awesome at your job.

Me: Don't make me roll my eyes.

Tyler: For one second, will you allow someone to praise you? Never mind. I'm calling.

A minute later, my phone rings and my heart sings only because I know Tyler's on the other line.

"Hey," I answer.

"How are you feeling, Gertie?" *FUCK!* It's Rachel.

"Oh, umm. Better, I guess."

"That's good. I just stopped by your room with Jennifer and you weren't in there. Just wanted to make sure you are okay."

"Uh, yeah. I umm, needed some fresh air."

"Oh, okay. Where are you? I'll come join."

"That's okay. I'm heading up soon anyway." I stand and brush myself off wanting to quickly get upstairs before she finds my ass a mess out here.

"Okay, well, feel better."

"Bye," I say before quickly hanging up hearing the beep on the other line, and I know it's Tyler. I wait a second to answer making sure Rachel's disconnected.

Taking a deep breath, I stare at the screen seeing Tyler's name and I smile.

"Hey there," I answer.

"Hey, yourself."

"How are you?" I ask.

"Well... I miss you so I'm not so sure I'm doing okay." He chuckles.

Softly, I reply, "I miss you, too."

"Gert?"

"Yeah?" I answer after a couple seconds.

"What's wrong?"

Through a sigh, "I don't know—"

"Gert, stop. Talk to me."

The sobs hit harder. "I think I want to come home sooner rather than later."

"Really?" His voice lights up.

"Yes, I realize I didn't just leave Gram behind. It was you, your family and our friends. I don't know what to do. You have your business there. I have my work here."

"Honey—" He sighs heavily.

"I know, I'm thinking too much."

He chuckles and I know he's reminiscing. "Do you know when you can take some time off?"

"I have a trip back here next week and then I was thinking about going home."

"Gertie! Are you seriously thinking that?" Tyler questions cheerfully.

"Yes, really." I laugh. I'm happy I got a chance to hear his voice.

"Mmm hmm. Damn, girl, I can't wait."

"Is that so?" I tease as the wind begins to pick up indicating a spring storm.

"What's that noise?" he questions confused.

"Oh, it's cars and the wind. This hotel is on a busy street."

"Uh, Gertie… Why are you calling from outside."

"Umm… I, uh… kind of lost it during a dinner meeting and needed fresh air." The line stays silent. "Tyler, I have spent the last year and a half making something of myself with the company and all was going great. I've moved up the ladder faster than most. I thought this was what I wanted but after seeing you... after spending time with you... I just..."

"You're not sure it's what you want now?"

"Yes, but, Tyler, it's crazy talk. I mean, come on. We spend two days together and it's as if we picked up where we left off years ago. As if we belong together."

Pause.

Longer pause.

Shit. Fuckity, fuck, fuck. Did I read *too* much into this?

He sighs heavily on the other end. "That's because we do."

Tears sting my eyes and I smile. Turning around, I look back at the hotel entrance. Is a corporate job really what I want? Or do I need what I long for—Eufaula's rivers, trees, and family gatherings? It was always my piece of heaven. My home.

But Mabel...

Twenty-One

"Why do humans get to go out walking the town, but if I do, I'm considered a nuisance? Seriously, humans litter all over the place as if the world is their trash can. At least my litter is biodegradable."

~Cujo

Gertie

Friday night with the girls. This is just what I need. I'm so freaking happy to have a weekend away from work. It's been one helluva week with the caddy bullshit Jennifer is full of and the too friendly boss. I can only pray this doesn't continue because it has me questioning whether I should even show up on Monday. Mabel tells me I need to hang tight and that things might get better. To give it time. I called Gram on my way home. She's excited about my visit. I didn't say anything to Rachel yet. I'll need to request my vacation time Monday morning. How can they say no? After the conference, I can edit Jennifer's article from any computer. I'm caught up on everything else and I have never—I repeat, never—taken time off. I go in sick or not. Crap, *now* I'm getting nervous with how Rachel will respond.

Gram told me to quit, and I made sure she knew her ever-loving mind was going. But, if things continue the way they did this week, I just might look for another job. Only thing is, it will have to be around here. There is no work for me in Eufaula and I refuse to work at the paper with Gram. She would be all up in my shit pressing me into things I'm not sure I'm ready for. Damn, if she didn't plant the seed, though.

"Woohoo! Free Friday. Gertie, you ready for some boot scootin' boogie?" Mindy sings coming in from the balcony after smoking a cigarette.

"Hell, yeah. Let's go!"

April, Leslie, Mindy, and I stroll down to our local honkytonk bar, The Lasso. It's not far from Chaps, in fact, just a block past.

"So, April, what's new?" I ask as we walk with our arms linked together.

"Not much other than work being a nightmare. We had our annual inspection and we failed. Now the doctor's ass is all over mine saying I should have fixed the shit I told him about months ago. It's his fucking practice. How the hell is it my fault?" She groans running her hands through her hair.

"That's messed up," Leslie quips cocking her head to the side.

April works as a manager for a local Neurologist. She's been there for a year and a half. April, with being one of his best employees, everything always falls on her shoulders.

"Yeah, I think I might start looking for another job if he can't get his head out of his ass," April retorts.

"Mindy, how are things with you?" Leslie asks trying to tame her hair.

"Same old, same old. Logan is doing awesome in school." She smiles holding her head high with pride. "Stupid teachers said he wouldn't be able to keep up with his peers in spelling. Little did they know, Logan is the king of repetition. I despise the stereotype they place on him. Just because he has Down's Syndrome doesn't mean he isn't smart. I hate it when I have to fight to add more goals on his educational plan. The kid is amazing, and they need to challenge him," she finishes shaking her head. I love how Mindy talks about her son. If only Jennifer could embrace awesomeness of her children rather than focus on the negativity.

"I have every bit of faith that you'll get the school straight," cheering her on, happy to be in the company of my best friends.

Strolling past Chaps, I give Sam a friendly wave and he shakes his head knowingly. He's aware of my Free Fridays and laughs every time I talk about it. I'm not a party person, but I love to get my boots out and let loose. I grew up line dancing back home with Gram at her crazy church gatherings.

"Leslie, what's new with you?"

"Well, honestly, not much. I've got Billy cutting teeth back home, so I can definitely use a night like tonight."

"Have you tried Old Grand-Dad?" I ask, pushing the small hairs blowing in the wind out of my face.

"You want me to give my child liquor?" Leslie gawks.

"Just put it on his gums. It will help numb the pain. It's not like you're putting it in his bottle, although he'd probably sleep through the night." We all laugh. "You know I'm kidding, right? Don't go make the little man an alcoholic at four months," I'm sure to add.

We finish catching up on our week by the time we reach The Lasso. Paying our cover, we head straight toward the bar weaving through the crowd to begin our first round of beers. The nice thing about country bars is you can actually have a conversation without screaming like you have to at some of those hip-hop clubs.

"Gertie, I think you need to hold off deciding whether to quit until after you go home. What if the town gossip is too much for you?" April questions compassionately.

"I don't know. If I had a week like yours, I'd me turning in my resignation letter as soon as possible," Mindy flattens in annoyance before taking a sip of her beer.

"No, I think I agree with April. You should wait," Leslie defends shaking her head.

"But I love my job. It's just the two new people I'm not happy with. I mean, yeah, one happens to be my boss and constant contact is a must. But, thank God, the other one works in another division." I sigh looking down at my beer.

Gulping another sip, Mindy chimes in, "Yeah, but what's that about looking into your resume? I've never heard of that. And do you know when this recognition is going to take place?"

I blink widely as I grasp how stupid I can be. "Uh... I kind of... never asked."

"What?" Mindy gasps loudly. "You just keep living in your happy little bubble, Gertie. Look how far it's gotten you." She raises her eyebrow in question.

I roll my eyes, grab my beer, and swivel around on the stool to watch the crowd. Most dress up trying to look the part. I, however, enjoy my braided pigtails, jeans, and plaid shirt tied at the waist. Some others dress like this, but then you've got the girls wearing glitter and shiny beads on their shirts and jeans. I never got into wearing flashy shit like that. It doesn't fit my personality.

Country Girl Shake It For Me by Luke Bryan begins to play instinctively pulling the four of us onto the wooden dance floor. I love line dancing because it helps me to keep the guys hands away as we move effortlessly in sequence changing walls or direction as most people say here in Houston. Those from small country towns like Eufaula speak the Nashville lingo. The song changes to *Boys Round Here* by Blake Shelton and the volte step kicks in.

We spend the majority of the night stomping, swaying, and shaking our bodies, mostly feet, until we're beyond tired. Saying our goodbyes, I let them know I might not be in town next week. Smiles light up the three faces as my eyes beam with enthusiasm. I can't wait!

Since it is eleven-thirty by the time I get home, I decide to send a text to Tyler in case he's sleeping.

Me: Goodnight, I love you.

Minutes slowly tick by without a response, and I decide to power off my phone and get a good night's sleep. Rick is arriving tomorrow, and I can only imagine the lectures and advice I'll be receiving.

Settled in my Pima and Egyptian cotton sheets, I drift off into a magical fairytale where Tyler and I live happily ever after.

Twenty-Two

"I get to see my cootie-freak human. Panting throughout the house, I can't contain my excitement, needing to smother her with kisses and watch her squirm. Why don't humans enjoy the simple things like us canine's do?" *smiling*

~ Cujo

Gertie

Loud pants and Mabel's squeal has me rolling my eyes as I walk down the hall to greet Rick. "And there's my baby girl," Rick says releasing Mabel from their hug. He reaches me in seconds, but Cujo's love has taken precedence.

"Hey, buddy. Wait! Noooo…" Cujo knocks me over on my rear and begins to lick my face giving me the heebie-jeebies.

"Cujo, behave," Rick asserts. I do love his dog. I've grown quite attached to the mutt even if he spends time slobbering and licking in places… never mind. *Ick!* I'm not going there. Rick picks me up twirling me around and I giggle like a two-year-old with their daddy.

Settling me on my feet, he asks, "Tell me, how are you?"

I smile without hesitation. "Good." Okay, I might be gleaming since I know Tyler and I are moving forward.

"It appears someone is a little more than just good," Rick announces increasing his volume with the word *good.* I smack his arm trying to get him to stop teasing me. "So are we ready?"

Rolling my eyes, I shake my head and walk back to my room. "Baby girl, you better get your dancing shoes on. Boots are not appropriate with this *Latin lover.*" I find him smirking when I turn around to argue because he owns a number of boots himself. Cujo follows me jumping on the bed finding his usual spot to curl up when he visits. "Don't take forever!" Rick hollers from the kitchen.

I decide ignoring Rick is best. He and Mabel begin yacking. I can tell they are pulling out the wine as glasses clink and clank. Music fills our apartment, and I know Rick is already taking over our playlist programmed on the extra iPod sitting next to our speaker system. I begin to hear *Bang, Bang* play and hurry with my shoes to get out there so the three of us can take our parts. Mabel takes Jessie J and I take on Ariana Grande while Rick rocks Nicki Minaj. We sing our hearts out using our wine glasses as our microphones, shaking our booties, prancing around and shooting each other the *bang bang.*

When the song is over, we clink our glasses quickly consuming the last drop. "Come on, ladies," Mabel says rinsing out our glasses. "Let's go." I give Cujo a pat on the head and tell him we'll be back. He'll be fine with his usual bowls already placed in the spot I made for when he comes to visit.

We have a cab take us to the club Rick loves, or shall I say, the club where Rick insists we go. Rick tugs my hand and I refuse, shaking my head. I need more liquid courage for what he's about to do. He rolls his eyes and takes Mabel. The guy loves to dance and I'm so thankful he does. When I was grieving over Tyler, Rick and I quickly became close because, well... he's like that fungus that grows and you can't get rid of it. He wouldn't leave me alone, visiting me at college as much as possible with his mutt. He loved forcing me to get up and go dancing. Since then, I've learned a lot of Latin moves.

Flagging the bartender, I order an orange juice and vodka, something I can drink quickly and will feel the effects almost as fast. It's only a matter of time until Rick pulls me to the dance floor.

Ricky Martin's *She Bangs* begins playing and I gulp my drink. Rick has a huge crush on the singer and will be pulling me out there again. I feel his hand rest on my lower back guiding me away from the bar. He doesn't even wait for me to set down my empty glass. I hand it to one of the nice patrons, who then hands it to the bartender.

Rick spins me around several times with my arm above my head and the warm liquid is helping me loosen up. I smile. He pulls me in, and we move our feet fast in rhythm with one another like we've done so many times. God, I love this guy. He spins me around while ruffling my skirt, teasing those around with our moves. Reaching for me again, he pulls me in and then out again while adding spins and a dip before bringing me up in a slow, seductive manner. If he wasn't gay, I would have snatched him up a long time ago.

Our mouths are open and just inches apart when I finally stand up. He spins me out with one arm to only bring me back in. Holding me close, he lifts one of my legs like they do on those dance shows. He holds onto my leg while he steps backward for a bit. My fingers are sprawled out on the outside of his shoulders and my head is turned to the side. We create a seductive pull between two characters. We continue the push and pull of two lovers ending with many spins and lots of footwork. So much that I'm sweating profusely. *Gross.* When the song is over, Rick wraps his arms around my waist and I follow suit. "You've become quite the dancer, baby girl," he whispers in my ear. Well, maybe he yells over the next song.

I pull him toward the bar where Mabel has ordered her drink. "Damn, you guys were amazing." Looking over at Rick, I smile knowing how much he appreciates comments like that. After all, it's because of him I can even make those moves. Thinking back to three years ago, I was horrible—talk about *two* left feet!

"I need another drink," I announce. We order drinks and Rick decides a round of shots is needed. I shake my head no. "Uh-uh. I don't drink those."

"Gertie, it wasn't the drinks that did it. It was the irresponsible driver. You are working on letting go of things with Tyler. It's time you get over this phobia, too." My eyes water and he leans in to hug me.

We clink glasses and, holy shit, that's gross! All liquored up, we head back to the dance floor. When Enrique Iglesias sounds through those magical speakers, I squeal and jump up and down like an idiot. But that's okay. If I can't have Rick as my Latin Lover, I'll take Enrique any day. As the sexy as hell singer sings for me to *Bailiando,* I do just that. Dance. The song moves through me down to my toes. Thanks to Rick, I now have a number of dances he helped me choreograph so that I don't always need a partner and this is one where I can use it.

I spin, fanning my skirt. Placing one foot in front of the other, I bend my knees slightly and clap my hands to the beating drum. Turning my trunk to the side, I rise, continuing to clap while my hips take on another move. I close my eyes as I feel the chorded strings pulsating through my veins. My arms move to each side along with my hips. I point my feet as they move from side to side. Spinning more, I find Rick smirking at me. He takes my hand, and we continue with our heads turned to opposite sides with chests pushed together, and our feet take over. Rick controls our movements and I happily oblige. I love dancing with him. The song finishes and I head back to the bar. This is one of my few nights I truly cut loose. Of course, it's when Rick comes to town. I've felt like he's been my rock ever since… Well, hopefully, I won't have to worry about that anymore.

"Mabel!" I scream when she comes to my side. "Want another drink?"

"Shots, more shots." She wiggles her eyebrows up and down knowing I'll do it because I have Rick here.

Turning to the bartender, I order three along with a glass of water. I have a feeling I should hydrate even though I don't want to. We tap our glasses together and down the burning liquid. *Blah!* Why the hell we're drinking this shit, I'll never know. I wish Tyler was here.

Hours later, and Lord knows how many drinks, I find the courage to go on the hunt for the DJ. I have a feeling Rick will love me after this. Mr. Hot DJ spins me around a bit to the song currently playing, places a kiss on my cheek, and assures me the song I requested is next. Excited, I head down to the dance floor because Rick is going to want me down there. I'm not sure how much more I'll be able to stand on these feet, so I better make my last dance worth it.

Trumpets and horns sound along with the bass guitar. Rick's eyes light up as if it is Christmas morning. He pulls me toward him and twirls me around in his arms. I lean my head back laughing. This is so much fun. He sets me down and we dance to his crush, Ricky Martin singing *Livin' La Vida Loca.* We sway our hips matching the others and Mabel joins. Dear God, my thighs are going to be sore.

The DJ talks over the music, "Work it, girl." I glance up and his eyes are checking me out. Ah, hell, I'll play, but I'm Tyler's now.

Uh, that admission has me pausing for a moment.

The next beat, my hips jiggle faster as I alternate swinging them from side to side and spinning. Once the song is over, I'm breathing hard and looking for water. My head spins and, holy shit, my feet hurt.

"Mabel, did you call a cab?" Rick asks. I can barely stand up.

"Oh, my gawd, you know what? I's neeeed to do something!" I interrupt the discussion about our ride home and explain. Their eyes grow for a second before smiling devilishly and agreeing to my crazy-ass idea.

"Rick, you're going to have to hold her down. She's Little Miss Prissy Pants."

"No, I'm nawt a pissy pants!" I shout at my sister. Rick and Mabel laugh.

"Gert, you're crazy! You know that, right?"

Laughing, I agree. "Yeah, but Tyla's gonna loooooooove it."

"I can't wait to see the look on his face." Rick laughs.

"You're both getting one, too," I demand.

"Hell fucking no!" Mabel shouts. "I want to enjoy watching you squirm under the needle. If I'm getting one, I can't do that, now can I?"

"Gertie, they don't always have more than one artist available. Ya know?" Rick tries to explain to my fuzzy brain.

"Rick, why are you gay?" Mabel asks, causing Rick and I to bust out laughing.

"Um... I don't know, Mabel. Why aren't you?" She shoves him into the taxi that's now arrived.

"You're a bitch. I meant, why couldn't you be straight? I'd so do you," Mabel admits.

"Oh, hell nooooo you can't. I saw him first. He's my fuuuuck buddy if he's anyone's—" I laugh.

"Fuck buddy? That's all I'd be to you?" Rick pretends to be upset.

"Yeah, because Tyler is the love of my life, and you would have been temporary until we could finally be together again. Ohhhhhh, but come here and give me a kiss, Ricky-poo, before I marry him." I pucker my lips up to him.

"No, you're ugly. I'd do Mabel before you."

"What?" I shout causing the driver to jump. "Oops." We giggle.

Arriving at the tattoo parlor, Rick asks, "So what is it going to say?"

"Tyler... *hello?!*"

"Aw, you're going to hurt Cujo's feelings. I could have sworn you would have chosen his name over Tyler's." Rick shakes his head sassily.

"Oh, my gawd, I would die if that slobbering messes' name was written on me."

"Can I help you?" the guy behind the counter asks.

"Uh, I'd like to get a tattoo."

"What do you have in mind?"

"I'd like my boyfriend's name."

Rolling his eyes. "Are you sure you aren't going to regret it later?" the guy asks.

"Excuse me?" I yell and then continue, "We've been together all our lives. Well, there was a three-year breakup—"

"Focus, Gertie! You don't have to tell the poor guy your life story," Mabel chimes in.

"Here, write his name so that the spelling is correct," the guy requests.

"Cujo," Rick whispers in my ear and then a "humph" when my elbow meets his stomach. "Damn, baby girl, no need to get violent. I was just joking."

"I'm getting Tyler, not Cujo, permanently marked on my skin to show him how much I loooove him," I slur.

Rolling his eyes, he says, "I'm going to be sick from your sappy shit. Write his name down and let's get this over with. I need to get back to Cujo before he pees on your bed."

I gasp. "He better not!" I turn back to the guy and write down the correct spelling. He has me follow him back and lay down on my stomach since I want the tattoo on my lower back.

The moment the needle hits, I nearly jump off the table. *Fuck, that hurts.*

"Hold on, let me help," Rick says rubbing my back trying to distract me. "So, you're going to marry Tyler?" Rick questions.

"Yep."

Mabel follows and watches the guy draw the name. "Oh, my God, Rick, look." Rick stops comforting me and the two begin to laugh hysterically.

"What? What's so funny?" I question. They can't talk from laughing so hard. "You better tell me what you're laughing at. The two look at each other and nearly spit on me as they laugh. "I'm going to kick your ass."

Mabel waves her hand in front of her trying to get her laughter under control. "It's nothing..." She falls over giggling. I roll my eyes and lay my head down praying this will be over soon. Damn thing burns.

The two bitches continue to snicker and sigh as they try to gain some sort of composure, but their efforts are futile. When the guy is finished, the drinks have hit their peak, and I want to just pay and get home before I vomit all over this place.

Stumbling to the waiting cab, we head home.

Twenty-Three

"A tattoo. Aw, I feel so special. This is cause to lick her. Come here, cootie-freak human."

~Cujo

Tyler

Holy shit. I hold my phone in disbelief. Rick swears it was a mistake, but damn. My Gert is going to be one pissed off red-head tomorrow.

I laugh and roll over in bed exhausted. Helping Ma clean out dad's side of the closet today was emotionally draining. Even though Gert's gonna be mad, I truly needed a good chuckle.

Twenty-Four

"Cootie-freak human says, 'Dog germs! Ew, ew, ew, ew, ew.'
But Mr. Prissy Pants cleans up my poop. I mean, really, Gertie?
He's the gross one."

~ *Cujo*

Gertie

My bladder wakes me screaming in dire need of relief as my head pounds as if the drummer is spotlighting his finale. Grabbing my head, I stumble out of bed. *Ouch!* Why the hell does my back hurt? The throbbing pain in my head takes over and I slowly crawl to the bathroom. My stomach begins to slosh around and I pause before climbing onto the toilet. Sliding down my shorts something gets caught. *What the hell?*

Oh, no, no, no, no!

What did I do?

My bladder continues to scream. I quickly finish relieving it and curiosity takes over while I stand grabbing the edge of the counter to steady my teetering vision. Turning my back to the full-length mirror behind the door, I scream, "OH. MY. GAWD! Mabel... Rick... Get your asses in here. NOW!"

Mabel comes running in and immediately breaks out into a fit of laughter.

"What is this?" I yell begging it to be temporary.

Snickering behind her hand to conceal her laugh, she says, "You wanted a tattoo."

"CUJO? Why do I have Cujo fucking tattooed on my rear, Mabel? How could you let me do this?" I shout as twinkle-toes makes his grand entrance. I start crying. "You let whoever did this permanently mark that flea-ridden critter on my ass?"

Rick turns the corner and joins Mabel's laughter. "Hey, now, don't talk about my baby like that! And he does not have fleas."

"I hate you both!" I spit and push past them retreating to my room to cry. What have I done? I need to Google how to get this thing removed. Grabbing my phone to text Tyler, I find messages from Rick. Oh, dear God. Images of last night's events begin to storm through my mind. I wrote down Tyler. So, why do I have Cujo's name and not Tyler's name on my back? Shit, Tyler's going to tease me.

Me: Morning.

Tyler: Hey, babe. You know it's not morning, right? How do you feel?

I now look at the time and find it's one in the afternoon. Yikes, how much did I have to drink last night? Ouch, my head.

Me: I'm never going out with them again!

Tyler: You don't love Cujo?

Me: THEY TOLD YOU?

Tyler: I got pictures, babe. ☺

Me: I'm going to crawl into a hole and die.

Tyler: Aw, babe. Rick told me what you wanted to be tattooed. I love you, sweetheart, but that's hilarious.

Me: I'm not talking to you again.

My phone rings almost instantly. "Hello?"

"Gert, please don't threaten me with that. I can't imagine ever not talking to you again." Tyler sighs sadly.

"I'm sorry," I whisper longing to feel his breath kiss my skin or his gentle touch painting my skin as if it were a canvas. Damn, maybe I'm still drunk from last night. "I didn't mean to upset you. I won't do it again, I promise," I confess a little louder forgetting the jackhammer attached to my head cursing a moan into my pillow. "Oh, wait, it's Sunday. I need to read Gram's column."

Tyler laughs deeply, and I can almost feel it through the line. "You'll get a kick out of it."

"Oh, dear, I can only imagine." Pausing for a moment to rub my eyes, "All right, I'm going to grab some coffee and check it out. I love you, Tyler."

"I love you, too."

Reaching over for my laptop, I decide to go directly to the bookmarked site where I'll find Gram's column and get coffee later.

Sunday, March 9, 2014
Drama Queens: Call Off Your Dogs

Citizens of Eufaula, Drama Mama here, and I'm going to tell you two pack-leading, alpha reads releasing this week.

If you are looking for a lick your paws, alpha read, look no further than Sarah's Call by Amy Togal. Amy takes you on a journey where a small-town girl, Anna, meets the big, rich, bad guy, Mike. Anna, weary at first, is quickly pulled into the curiosity that is Mike and what he wants to do. She has no idea the lifestyle he leads and winds up running from him scared. What Mike didn't anticipate was falling in love with the one girl he was supposed to tarnish. Is it possible for Anna to survive this? Can Mike leave what he was supposed to do behind and follow his heart or will he continue onto his next victim?

Another alpha-submissive read hitting shelves this week is Tina Neal's Interpretations. Tina introduces the strong male, Lucas, who everyone drools over, but is untouchable. He chooses everything in life very carefully. Clothing, furniture, even down to the women he takes home. Picky doesn't begin to describe his personality. Tina brilliantly brings in Laura, a top executive for a Fortune 500 company, who undoubtedly didn't ask for a lifestyle that Lucas painted for her. After numerous requests by the one and only Lucas Berabone, she lets down her guard and finds not only an adventure, but also, the possibility of true love. Will she let herself explore new opportunities or will she shut everyone out and continue the path that is familiar?

Okay, kittens. I'll never lead you astray, tie you up to a chain or put you down because I've got some poop to scoop this week! We all know dogs are, by their very nature, loyal, empathetic, and full of personality. When in a pack, there is order and communication, everyone follows suit and there is no drama. Humans can be very dumb and selfish creatures. Most of us don't communicate like adults and that's when you need to get a dog trainer to come in— stat! Those people know their stuff.

What's sad is in the Indie Author world, it's a dog eat dog world. Misguided, impressionable people don't view it as a need to see the dog trainer. They'd much rather become aggressive. When I say aggressive, I don't mean the baring teeth, snarling, and growl behavior like most associate with a vicious dog. No, this is a competition. Everyone looks out for themselves and they don't follow the pack hierarchy that keeps everyone in check. This behavior, with the proper dog trainer, could be cured. Say, for instance, authors who have made friends with those they use for editing, formatting, and cover art—that's a big no-no because what authors don't realize is these friends won't always have their back, especially if they are an author themselves. They will, at any chance, use the work of others to get ahead. In a dog pack, the alpha not only is the head-honcho, but also will do everything in its power to take care of those who have given trust to the alpha. These so-called self-serving friends in the Indie Author world are not leaders who you should willingly give trust. They are most likely going to cause collateral drama.

There it is, pups. Drama Mama's paw print. Until next week, keep your eyes open for those caustic behaviors in humans around you and thanks for reading Drama Queens: Call Off Your Dogs.

I shake my head in disbelief. Gram's the kind of woman whose heart is full of words that make her the loving person who raised me, but also the pain in the ass that dredges stuff up like this to piss people off. All the while, she sits back wearing a smirk. She truly enjoys this. I just know it.

My door squeaks open. "Chica?" Ricks asks testing my mood.

"Yes?" I respond before the four-legged lump of love jumps on my bed and licks me incessantly. "Cujo, stop trying to kiss my face!" His strength is so great that I can't believe how sweet he is. He could take down anyone. I toss my head back and forth trying to outsmart the thing while my head continues to retaliate.

"Baby girl, can we talk?" Rick asks lying down next to me on the bed. "Cujo, settle down," he asserts and the damn thing listens to him, but not me. *Argh!*

I sigh settling into my covers. "Yeah."

"Can I ask what you're doing?"

"What do you mean? I'm lying next to you." I crinkle my forehead immediately regretting it.

"I'm talking about Tyler."

"How long have you been talking to Tyler?"

"Excuse me, baby girl. Stop the transference. We aren't talking about me. This is about you."

I close my eyes. "I don't understand your question."

"He loves you—in fact he never stopped. Do you realize when you ran away three years ago, you ran away from everything? You haven't been back once, not even to visit your parents' grave. I'm not telling you that you have to go home." He pauses to look me square in the eyes. "What I want is for you to open yourself up and see reality for what it is. You hide from everyone using work as an excuse." I gasp and immediately want to interject. He places a finger on my lips to shush me. "Be honest with yourself if no one else. Are you truly happy where you work? Is this job going to be the one who stands by you when you need someone?"

Tears saturate my pillow. "I have Mabel, Gram, and you." I pause to think. "What are you doing, Rick?"

His hand brushes my hair away from my face and lovingly strokes my head. "I want you happy. That's all I've ever wanted. So when are you getting married?"

My eyes grow. "What? I'm not marrying Ty! We just got back together."

"That's not what you said last night." He stops and lays back. "Isn't that right, Cujo?"

"No!" Cujo immediately inches his way between us as he licks his chops. "I was drunk out of my mind. I plead the fifth on anything I did and said. I mean, for heaven's sake, Cujo is on my ass."

Rick and I laugh and enjoy catching up. How he's analyzing every one of my responses doesn't go unnoticed.

Twenty-Five

"Humans are strange creatures. I'll live just a small percentage of their life and not ask one question, yet they question everything. Maybe that is the key to longevity. Now, how do I go about asking one of those questions? Hmm..."

~ *Cujo*

Gertie

Monday morning, earbuds plugged and I'm strutting down the street in heels thanks to my bright idea of leaving my tennis shoes behind. I curse myself for being so foolish.

My flight leaves tomorrow morning for my three days of hell. Well, not really hell, *hell*. Just the company I'll be keeping. I'm actually excited about the event.

Me: Good morning. Putting in for vacation next week.

Tyler: I can't wait to see you again!

Me: I miss you.

Tyler: I miss you, too. Gotta go. I love you.

Me: I love you, too! xoxo

With my mind bouncing with thoughts of going home, a mile walk seems strangely short.

"Good morning," Penny greets.

"Good morning to you too, Penny," I reply as I head to my desk performing my usual ritual—unload my backpack and remove the smell of outside with a spritz of perfume. Of course, my ritual was messed up a bit since I didn't have to change shoes. A knock on my door halts any further productivity.

"Hello, Gertie. I didn't hear from you all weekend," Rachel greets a little too straight forward. *Uh, excuse me?*

"I… umm… had plans with family and friends."

"Oh, I see." She clucks.

"Yeah, about that. I wanted to give you a heads up first that I'm requesting time off next week."

"You can't do that," Rachel immediately responds.

"Why not?" I ask shocked.

"Company policy says you must give a two-week notice for any personal days or vacation time."

"Rachel…" I begin, "I've never taken a day off since I began working here, even during my internship in college. I work hard. I can help Jennifer with the story while I'm away. I don't understand why it's a big deal."

"Corporate policy." She shrugs.

My vision blurs and I feel like a weight has just fallen on my world. *What a fucking bitch!*

Quickly, I reply, "Well, I'm giving two-week notice for vacation right now." I turn toward my laptop and power it on. She must understand my irritation by the diluted conversation and then she walks out without even a goodbye.

The rest of the day, I sit brooding at my desk unable to concentrate on much. I'm so pissed. Rachel acts like my best fucking friend, and then one week later turns into a bitch. I should have known that was coming. Red flags were everywhere and even Mabel warned me. Irritated, I reach for my water knocking it over on my keyboard. *Fuckity, fuck, fuck, fuck, fuck.*

I make quick work drying my laptop. Oh, no, the spacebar isn't working. This cannot happen. I turn my laptop over and bang the underside, hoping CPR-infant-style will do the trick. A few droplets fall onto my desk. That's it. Maybe it will work now. *Dammit, it's ruined.*

Add that to my piss-poor mood and I'm calling it a day. Grabbing everything and changing into my tennis shoes, I pass a concerned Penny, who's thankfully busy on the phone. Slapping down a sticky note saying, "See you next week," I walk out. I mean, come on, it's three-thirty.

The elevator chimes and I walk in before stopping dead in my tracks. *Rachel.*

"Leaving so early?" She raises her eyebrow. *Fuck you, bitch.*

"Yeah, everything is done," I lie. "Going shopping for a couple dresses before tomorrow."

"Oh, okay. Well, then, I'll see you in the morning." She walks out of the elevator she had propped open with her hand. "Don't be late," were her final words before the doors close. I can't help it—both my middle fingers fly up telling her exactly what I think of her and that company policy shit.

Scrolling through my playlist, I find something that helps rid my anger as I walk home. I cannot believe this bullshit. I have never taken a day off, and the one time I actually want to do something, I can't go when I want. My hair blows in the wind as I pass people who are out and about enjoying the warm weather. It appears the poor flowers adorning storefronts didn't suffer too much from last week's unseasonable cold spell. At least they aren't suffering.

Shit, I need to text Tyler. I hope I don't disappoint him.

Reaching the apartment, Rick and Mabel are deep in conversation, but jump when the door closes. Mabel immediately looks at her watch in confusion. See, I *am* a workaholic. Cujo approaches and the comfort of his greetings warm my heart. Misty-eyed, I quickly stand and rush down the hall. I need to get to my room.

"Gert?" Rick calls out, but I ignore him. Cujo jumps on my bed. Dropping my bag, I curl up with him. This is what I want. I want to come home to someone greeting me like this. *Tyler*. I want Tyler.

Sobs erupt and Cujo licks my hand every time I stop rubbing his body. Damn dog is so demanding. Maybe he's helping to distract my sadness.

A knock sounds and Cujo's head perks up as if protecting my fragile state. "Baby girl?" I shake my head into the covers wanting him to go away. Of course, he has to be as demanding as his dog. "What happened?" I roll over to talk knowing he's going to get his way. "Ew, wait a minute." He reaches over for a tissue. "Such a petite flower," he retorts sarcastically. I roll my eyes.

"Seriously, baby girl, what has you so upset?" He waits patiently while I blow my nose. "Did you quit?" he asks a little too expectantly.

"Go away," I shove him causing him to slide off the bed giving me a much-needed laugh. "No, I didn't quit."

"Damn." My eyes bug out at his response. "What?" He shrugs. "You don't belong here—give this poor guy a break."

"Shut up. No, I told Rachel I planned to go home next week, and she told me corporate policy requires a two-week notice for things like that." I air quote.

"Okay, did you know this policy?"

"No, Rick! I've never taken time off before."

"Well, there's your problem—hiding in your work." This grants him another eye roll. I'm tired and could really use Tyler's arms to hold me.

"And I spilled water on my laptop, and I'm not sure if it will work again. The spacebar isn't working and I don't know what else." I weep hiding my face, and maybe the world, in Cujo's neck.

Rick laughs. "Don't you know you shouldn't have opened containers around those things?" He pushes my back. "Here," he pulls my laptop out of my backpack, "put your password in, and I'll have a look." I do as he says and fall back next to Cujo, whose breath reeks of ass. *Ack!*

Sitting up, I watch Rick mess around with the laptop holding practically my entire work-life.

"Well, good news and bad news."

"Bad first."

"Typical Gert style," Rick mumbles under his breath. *Asshole.* "You have a number of keys that double, but your spacebar is now working."

"Okay, and the good news?"

"The spacebar is working," he says dryly.

"Fuck! What do I do?"

"Order a new keyboard or buy a new laptop," he stops, "but knowing the cheap ass girl you are, I suggest you get a new keyboard."

I gasp. "How dare you."

"Oh, stop. You know I only say it like I see it." He smirks closing the laptop.

"Are you planning to stay here the entire time I'm in DC?"

"Hell, yeah. We're partying it up while you're gone. Don't get upset if you come home to the apartment trashed." He runs his hand along my bedspread. "You might want to order a new bed set, too. Lord knows how crazy we'll get." Groaning, I roll my eyes and lay back down. Cujo lifts his head again.

"What's going on in here?" Mabel chimes.

"We're talking about all that partying that's going on when she finally leaves tomorrow." Rick wiggles his eyebrows. I grab a pillow and throw it at him.

"Crap, I need to go buy some dresses." Mabel and Rick's eyes light up. "Fine, but I need to hurry up because I've got to call and tell Tyler."

"Tell Tyler what?" Mabel asks. Thankfully, Rick fills her in.

Twenty-Six

"Happiness isn't buying me a new toy, but I beg of you not to tell Mr. Prissy Pants because he'll stop bringing them home. No, happiness is the little things—like getting your belly rubbed by one of your favorite humans."

~ *Cujo*

Tyler

I can barely breathe from the shocking excitement. Holy fucking shit, she wants to come home. I don't know whether to jump up and down or scream, but then I'll wake up the house. Crap. I had better get busy on that dock. I can't wait to show her.

The next morning, I'm up before my alarm sounds.

I need to call Ma.

"Hello?" she answers quietly. I wonder if she's having trouble, accepting dad's gone. I can't imagine losing the one I love. That would kill me.

"Ma, I have great news."

"Wow, Tyler, whatever it is has put a spring in your voice like it used to…"

"She's coming home."

"What? Oh, Tyler, when?"

"I don't know for sure. She's hoping to make it next week."

"I am so happy for you. Keep calm, honey. I'm sure you're scared how she'll react, but honestly, Tyler, we all know Gertie and it will be fine, son."

"I hope you're right."

"Sweetheart, I have an idea. Come to the house tomorrow. There's something your dad and I wanted to give to you this summer, but…"

"How are you holding up?"

"Oh, sweetheart, the little pitter-patter keeps my heart beating strong."

I chuckle lightly. "I know what you mean."

"I'll be over after my morning check-in. Love you, Ma… and…." I take a deep breath, "please know I'm here."

"Of course, honey. I'll see you in the morning." We hang up, but not before I hear her sniffle a cry. My heart hurts for Ma. She and dad were high school sweethearts and celebrated their thirty-first wedding anniversary last fall. Thank heavens they were blessed with the time they had. And that's what I want. I don't want to waste time knowing Gert is the one all along and then us to be apart.

Time escaped my parents. I can't let any more time be snatched from me and the love of my life.

I lay back on the bed. My Gert's coming home. Suddenly, my stomach falls. What if? Dammit, I need to just let it be. I have this time to finish putting the final touches on the house and to get the dock built. That is... if nothing else happens. The spring weather brings colds. It can't be good for her. I need to do everything in my power to make sure she stays well.

After morning chores and drop offs, I sit at my desk to go through message after message making sure no one's fucking up with the inspector's again. I gave each crew shit for last week. I can't have the inspectors crawling up my ass again. They're liable to shut down sites if that's the case or worse—begin nitpicking more.

"Good morning," Greg says walking into my office trailer. The biggest job I have right now, besides getting Gertie back and keeping someone healthy, is a private clubhouse on the south side of the lake. We've already made the renovations necessary to bring the hotel into the twenty-first century. Now they want to add a clubhouse exclusive to guests who stay at the current luxury hotel, along with a waterfront restaurant. It's something I'm very proud of. One of the few sites inspectors haven't bitched about. This is definitely going to be the highlight of my portfolio.

"Morning," I respond with enthusiasm.

"Wow, something's going on to have that smile back."

"What the hell does that mean?" I question as my forehead puckers.

"Dude, you haven't worn a smile like that in years."

I laugh. "Gertie's coming home."

"No way! When?" Greg asks surprised as he leans against the wall.

"Next week."

"How did you manage that one?" his eyes gleam of deviltry as he twirls his keys around.

I throw a pen at my cousin who quickly catches it before it hits his head. "Fine, don't tell me. I just stopped by to let you know I sent a crew over to your house."

"You got the plants I specified?"

He rolls his eyes. "Yes, I got everything on the list, and we'll have it all prettied up in time for Gertie's arrival. The sod isn't coming in until Friday, though."

I nod. "That's okay. As long as it gets done before she arrives." I pause looking up at Greg, who seems to be distracted. "What's up with you?"

"I talked with your mom. She told me what happened. You okay?"

"Yeah, I think so. I signed the papers for them to proceed. The doctor says he thinks it will work." I sigh heavily.

"Sweet, you guys deserve some good news after everything."

"I agree. What's up with you? Are you still seeing Amber?"

"No, that ship sailed."

"What the hell?"

"Dude, I have no interest in settling down anytime soon."

"Whatever!"

"Remember, I'm not the pussy-whipped one. I can't stand it when girls get all clingy and shit. I don't know why they don't listen when I tell them there is no future with me. But, damn, if they don't start talking about the future anyway. Pisses me the hell off."

"Dude, you aren't getting any younger. Don't you want to have a family? You're four years older. It's about time you grow a pair and stop running away from your commitment issues."

"Fuck you!"

"No, go talk to Rick about that. I'm sure you guys can work something out." Quickly, the pen hits my chest and we both laugh while Greg settles on the sofa. I ordered a sofa for the office trailer for long nights working that sometimes leave me passed out with my head in awkward positions on the desk. I always woke up with a kink in my neck and a stiff back. The sofa is supposed to remedy that from happening again. Unfortunately, with all that's happened, dad's death, Gertie, and...

"Hey, Pansy! Where'd you go?"

Oh shit, I zoned out. "I just have a lot on my mind."

"Hmm mmm, I'm sure you do. So, anyway, your yard will be finished by the end of next week. I need to head over there and make sure they are following your layout."

I look him square in the eye. "Please tell me Mike isn't on the job."

"I don't know what your problem is with him. He's one of my hardest workers."

"He's an asshole."

"Pfft, so are you!"

"Yeah, but that guy has issues that just bug the shit out of me."

"He does not."

"Whatever, go! I need to work."

"See ya later, Pansy." I throw the pen at his retreating form and, unfortunately, hit the door as he's walking out. I can hear his loud booming laughs all the way to his truck. *Asshole.*

The day runs with the normal problems that spring up needing to be resolved. It's the nature of the business. I can't wait to get out of here, though. A renewed sense of excitement has me wanting to work on the dock. I doubt I'll have it finished for this summer, but I'm going to try my hardest.

The phone rings. "Hello."

"Tyler. How are you doing, darling?"

"I'm good, Gram. How are you?" I ease back in my chair and begin to swivel around in circles.

"Great!" she responds sounding somber. "Well, I was just wondering... you know..."

"What are you trying to pull now?"

"Tsk. Why must you think so ill of me?" I roll my eyes. Gram is up to something.

"You know I don't think of you like that. Cut to the chase. What's going on?"

"Oh... I was just checking in to see if you talked to...."

"Yes, I spoke to Gert." She gasps excitedly at my response.

"And..." she eggs on.

"How about you call Gert and find out? I have a stack of papers to go through before I go home."

"I don't know what I'm going to do with the two of you."

"Gram, she agreed to come home for a visit. It's not like I can tell her to come home permanently."

"No, boy, but when she sees..."

"I'm scared to death."

"Oh, you have nothing to worry about there. I've known all along that it will work out. Go do your paperwork, boy. I'll check in later."

"Bye, Gram."

"Toodaloo!" She hangs up and I spin around to throw my head onto my arms. I'm not going to lie—I'm scared out of my mind. The very thing I need to show her might send her running away again. And I just can't let that happen.

Sitting in a rocking chair, I take a sip of my beer gazing at the sky wondering what Gertie's up to.

Her ringtone sounds and I smile.

"Hey, babe."

"Tyler?" Gertie sounds as if she's crying.

"What's wrong?" Her demeanor has me sitting up straighter.

"Rachel won't let me take off until the week after next."

I close my eyes and will away the building sadness. Taking a deep breath, I tell her, "It will be okay. You're coming home, right?"

"Yeah, but... I really miss you," she says through tears.

"I know. I miss you like crazy, too." I sigh not wanting to tell her how much it hurts me, too. "It's one more week. I'm sure the time will fly by with your trip, and then you'll have a week to make plans on who you want to see while you are home." If I have any confidence in my voice, I should fucking receive an Oscar because it's definitely not the way I'm feeling. *Fuck, another week?*

"Mom can't wait to see you."

"Really?" she begins to cheer up. "I miss her so much."

"I know, babe. She feels the same way."

"Tyler…" There's a pause, "I'm sorry I ran."

"Gert," I pause to catch my breath, "don't be sorry. We can't fix what's been done. We can only fix the here and now." Again, that should be fucking Oscar-worthy right there.

"You're one smart hottie." She laughs.

"Oh, I'm a hottie, am I?" I playfully question.

Damn, I miss her. It was one thing to have the possibility of us working things out hanging over me for years but after seeing her, being with her, every second feels like fucking hell.

Two weeks.

It will be torture, but I can do two weeks.

Maybe.

Twenty-Seven

"I heard I'm adopted. What does that mean exactly?"

~ *Cujo*

Gertie

I board the plane still pissed off. Tyler assured me one more week won't kill us. I'm not sure I agree with him. It *is* already killing me.

Rachel, Adam, and Jennifer are keeping to themselves. I don't know what the hell is up everyone's ass. I'm the one pissed. Jennifer can suck my big toe if she has a problem writing the article.

I open my laptop and decide to type a quick email to Tyler.

From: Gertie Sawyer
To: Tyler Jackson
Date: 11 March 2014 7:40 A.M.
Subject: I miss 5you

Pardobn the t5ypos. Water has ruibned m5y ke5ybnoard. I ordered obne last bnight, bnut it wobn't arrive ubntil Frida5y. Good bnews, it seems to bne obnl5y four ke5ys messed up. I hope 5you cabn ubnderstabnd this. Have a great da5y. Call 5you tobnight.

Love 5you.

Gert

I hit send before the plane takes off.

"So, are you excited?" I look up and see Rachel addressing me. Preoccupied from thoughts of Tyler, I cock my head to the side to study her for a minute.

I shrug my shoulders. "Yeah."

"Where exactly are you going on vacation?"

"Home."

"Where is that… Oklahoma?"

"Yes."

"Gertie, those small towns can be damaging to career-oriented people like you and me." *What?*

I give her a look that, hopefully, shuts her mouth. *Highly doubt it.*

"They are small-minded people who litter your mind with farming, family, and church, and they have no direction."

"I don't know where you got that information, but I can assure that you are indeed wrong. Eufaula is nothing like that, and I'm not really sure there are many places on earth like the place you just described, if they even exist." I try to defend people I don't know to this closed-minded woman.

"Well, as your friend—"

"I'm not your friend, Rachel. I am your employee," I voice before pulling my headphones out and turning up the music. Her jaw seemingly clenches. Guess I hit a nerve. *Oops.*

I close my eyes and lean my head back. Done. That's what I am.

Done.

If it weren't for the convention and how many others who are depending on me, I might have the audacity to file a complaint. She has stepped over the line since day one and I am done.

Done.

Hours later, we grab our luggage and proceed to the waiting limo. *Of course.* The company doesn't have the money to spend so that I'm not a fucking hostess, but we have the money to throw at a limo? *Bitch.*

"Gertie, I need you in the lobby ready to go at five. Okay?" Rachel breaks the silence.

"I'll be there." I respond pulling out my cell to text Tyler.

Me: Landed and on the way to the hotel.

Tyler: Glad to hear. You okay?

Me: Yes, just waiting for this trip to be over.

Tyler: I know sweetheart. Chin up. You'll be great.

Me: Thank you. I'm not sure I'll have time to message you until late or maybe tomorrow.

Tyler: Try to have fun, Gert. Love you.

Me: Love you, too! xoxo

I put away my phone just in time to reach the hotel. I do everything I can to steer clear of everyone in fear I'll blow a gasket.

"Gertie, I'm sorry if I upset you. That was not my intention. I just don't want you to get clouded with whatever has you wanting to go home. Apparently, there is something bothering you in your personal life that is beginning to make you lose focus, and I would hate for it to affect your job," Rachel instructs me as we ride together to Memorial Continental Hall.

"I understand," are the only words I'm able to form as a response. I can sense the back of my eyes are becoming heavy. Showing the bitch she got to me is the last thing I want to do with this woman. She *can't* know how much her statement hurts.

"Well, the docents have everything in place. We'll do a quick walk through and watch over during the cocktail party to make sure everyone is enjoying themselves."

"Okay." My attention remains on the busy streets and not Rachel while I beg my mind to think of something else. It's no use, though. She truly got to me.

We arrive and do the stupid inventory. I try to stay focused, but for some reason I can't. I don't know how to deal with the mixture of emotions going on inside of my head right now. Running far away sounds like heaven at this moment.

"Guests should be arriving in minutes," Rachel tells the docent.

"We have everything ready and don't foresee any problems. The guest list can easily be accommodated," the docent responds. *See, bitch! Not my fucking job.*

"Very good. Gertie, let's have a toast," Rachel declares cheerfully grabbing two flutes. "To tonight and many more." We clink glasses and I guzzle the champagne. "Whoa! Easy, girl. We can't have you drunk while Simple Luxury is on display, now can we?"

Whatever! I do my best to ignore the ignorant woman.

"Good evening," a gentleman, whom I remember very well, greets Rachel.

"Oh, Peter, it's so nice to see you. Peter, this is Gertie Sawyer, one of our editors with Simple Luxury." She turns to me, "Gertie, this is Peter Fox, the owner of Williams."

"Why, yes, Gertie. How are you this evening?" Peter directs to just me taking my hand in his and kissing the back of it. I blush.

"Do you two know each other?" Rachel asks placing a hand on her hip.

"Oh, you didn't know about my internship at Williams? I believe it's on my resume," I quickly retort throwing in that dig with her snooping around with my resume.

"Oh… why… umm… yes, I did." She fumbles over her words.

"Rachel, you should really work on your communication skills," I unprofessionally suggest to my boss causing her to gasp and walk away.

"How are things with you, Peter?"

"Good. Glad to see you're still the strong Gertie we knew last year."

"Haven't changed a bit." I smile proudly.

"You know, I always have a spot open at Williams with your name on it," he states.

"I know," I say shaking my head playfully. "You know I wanted to make it on my own. I didn't want any handouts."

"Just as foolish as always," Peter jokes. "I better go find my wife before she thinks you stole me again."

"Oh, how is Hannah?"

He chuckles. "Ready to pop." Just then, she turns the corner with a very round belly. "One more month," Peter whispers.

"Congratulations!" I exclaim walking toward the very pregnant woman I liked from the minute I met her years ago. "Oh, Hannah, you look beautiful," I tell her wrapping my arms in a genuine embrace around the wife of my old boss.

"Thank you. I tell you, Gertie, finding a dress that fits me right now was like finding a needle in a haystack." She laughs.

All too quickly, the room fills. We say our goodbyes and I search for another flute. Last week, Rachel told me to have fun tonight and I plan to do just that.

The evening continues where I mingle with so many influential people that I'm almost star-struck. I still can't believe I'm here attending the convention, much less sharing the same air with these amazing people. Thank heavens for champagne.

Rachel has been absent since she supposedly, in her mind, introduced me to Peter. Funny how she thought I didn't know who he was or the very company he started. Feeling the buzz of alcohol, I smile thankfully. It just might be what I need to get through tonight. Maybe if I stay tipsy over the next couple days, I'll leave Washington, DC with my sanity still intact. *Damn Rachel and her pet for tarnishing this experience.*

"Gertie!" Adam scrambles in panic.

"What?" I ask worried something happened with the cocktail mingle.

"It's Rachel. She had an encounter with someone she used to work with and is a mess. I need you to go check on her."

"Where is she?"

"On the Portico." I roll my eyes after he tells me. I'm not a fucking babysitter. Now I have to go take care of a grown woman? What the hell... more drama? She's one of the last people I want to help after what she said about my hometown.

Exiting the building, I spot Rachel sitting to the side crying. *Seriously?*

"Everything okay?" I ask making sure there is distance between us. I don't want to console her. How many times in the last week have I been upset, but remained professional?

"It was just," she heaves heavy for a breath, "seeing her..." Sob... "brought back all the memories and how she did me wrong." She sobs harder throwing her arms around my neck. *For the love of all that is holy!* My hands don't know what to do. Hesitating, I slowly pat her back making me very uncomfortable. No comforting embrace to give here.

"Well, I'll go back and make sure everything runs smoothly," I suggest as I try to get away.

"I..." hiccup, "appreciate your help." She hiccups again. *Help?* Didn't she say... oh, never mind. I don't care enough right now.

With another quick pat on her back, I step away. "Okay, I'll see you," I quip just before turning around and wanting to run for dear life. Oh, my, I can almost feel a smile begin to form. *This is so messed up.* Your boss falls apart at this amazing function and you have to not only pick up her job, but are also asked to fucking babysit her? *Screw that! I need more champagne.*

Returning to the Banquet Hall, I find Jennifer and fill her in. She surprisingly says she'll help out. Wow, maybe I was wrong about her. A docent walks by with a tray of champagne flutes. I grab one and walk out onto the balcony to take a moment to get over my irritation.

The Washington Monument is lit up and the sight is breathtaking. I could spend the rest of the evening out here. Stars are out, but the surrounding lights pollute their presence. A slight breeze blows the wisps of hairs I left out of my typical up-do. I close my eyes and think of home.

Tyler.

I wonder what he's doing right now.

"Gertie?" *Oh no! Please, go away.*

"Yes, Adam?" I answer curtly keeping my back to him. *So much for peace.*

"How is she?"

"She's a big girl and doesn't need me to help her through whatever is going on."

"Oh, I see," he says with his breath on my neck.

"What are you doing?" I lift my arm to get his smug breath off me, turn around, and back away.

"Come on, Gertie. Don't be like that."

"Be like what? I'm not interested, Adam!" Hopefully, the annoyance is prevalent in my voice.

"That's not what it felt like a week and a half ago."

"Adam, I have only ever loved one man and I plan to spend the rest of my life loving only that man. There will be no one else." I begin to walk back inside when he grabs my arm.

"It wouldn't be wise to turn me down." His stare turns hard and cold.

"Are you threatening me?" I spit yanking my arm out of his hand.

"It's not a threat... it's...."

"OH, MY GOD!" I scream and run into the crowd. *How stupid am I?* I don't need this. Tears build and I allow them to fall freely.

"Gertie, are you okay?" Jennifer asks with wide eyes. She reaches out to hold me still.

"No!" I look over my shoulder and see Adam's stern glare. "I have to go." I turn back to Jennifer, who looks like she's trying to calculate what's going on. I need to get out of here.

Fuck Adam.

Fuck Rachel.

Fuck work.

Knowing the stairs are quicker, I run. Heels clank with every step. Reaching the entrance, I pass shocked and concerned guests. I must look a mess. Rachel calls out, but I don't respond. I continue down the stairs and raise my hand to one of the waiting cabs. Luckily, I had some extra room in my dress to store my cell phone. Telling the cab driver where to take me, I call Tyler. It rings and rings. No answer.

I call Rick next. "Hi, baby girl." He sounds exhausted.

"Rick... sorry to wake you. But... I'm... uh... I'm done. I've quit."

"Wait! You didn't wake me. What happened?" he demands. *Him and his fucking demands.*

"I don't have time to tell you. I need to call the airline and get a flight."

"Okay, call me back, please. I love you."

"Love you, too."

Opening the app on my phone, I search and find the first flight into Tulsa is leaving in two hours. It's the closest major airport. Damn thing has a four-hour layover, but it will get me there. Booked, I step out of the cab and make a run for my room. I need to pack and get to the airport. I bribed the man to wait for me with a hundred dollar bill. If he leaves, I'm kicking his ass. Well, no not really. I don't have time for that.

Five minutes later, I'm settled in the taxi dressed in yoga pants, a sweatshirt, and flip-flops. My dress is probably ruined in my haste to pack, but I don't care. I'm not sure if I'll ever need it again. I call Tyler again, and there's still no answer.

Plugging in my headphones, I lose my thoughts to the music streaming through my headphones. Finally, a little peace.

Once I'm checked in at Dulles airport and through security, I open my laptop and type one of the hardest things I've ever done.

From: Gertie Sawyer
To: Matt Edwards, CEO
Time: 11 March 2014 10:37 P.M.
Subject: Resigbnatiobn

It is with deepest regard that I must resigbn as editor for Simple Luxur5y effective immediatel5y.

Gertie Saw5yer

Damn keyboard.

I hit send before I lose my will to do what is right. To do what is needed.

Oh, shit. I don't have a job now.

Fuck, I think I'm going to hyperventilate.

Twenty-Eight

"Mr. Prissy Pants is jumping around making me dizzy. Someone, call the vet. He needs Xanax—stat."

~ *Cujo*

Gertie

I finally arrive in Eufaula after driving over an hour from the Tulsa airport. It's nearly morning. We have a small airport in town, but it's mainly small airplanes running in and out. You have to know someone with a plane to catch something spur of the moment like this unless I wanted to spend a fortune. Then, by the time the plane is fueled and ready, I'd be in Eufaula anyway. Renting a car was the easiest solution.

I've sent texts to Rick and he has yet to respond. Tyler's not answering his phone and neither is Gram. I have no clue where everyone is. Then again, it's the crack ass of dawn. I can't call Rick, he's in Houston and probably asleep. Crap, I need to call Mabel. At least she won't beat my ass for waking her up.

"Hello?" Mabel answers half asleep.

"Mabel, I left. I'm about four miles away from Grams and I can't get ahold of Tyler, Rick, or Gram. Can you wake Rick? I need to tell him something."

"Wait! Hold up, slow down. Damn, Gert. I hate it when you babble. Why are you in Eufaula?"

"I quit."

"What?! And you didn't tell me?"

"There was no time. Seriously, Mabel. Can I please talk to Rick?"

"Uh... he left earlier today."

"I thought he was staying with you." I try to process my thoughts. "But I talked to him earlier."

She sighs heavily. "You probably talked to him while he was driving home."

"Is something wrong?"

"Okay, Gertie. There is something you don't know. Please don't be mad."

"Mabel, what the hell? Spill it, I'm kind of freaking out here. I'm jobless and can't get ahold of anyone but you."

"Well, jeez, I love you, too."

"Mabel..." I warn.

"Fine. You need to turn around and go to the hospital."

"The hospital?!" I yell.

"Calm down. I can't tell you any more than that. I'll try to get ahold of Rick and have him meet you at the entrance to the emergency room because the main doors are still closed at this hour."

"Mabel?" I begin to cry. "What happened? Is Gram…"

"NO! Sweetie, listen to me. Take a deep breath. I need you to promise me that you will remain calm and keep yourself strong for Tyler."

"Tyler! Oh, my God, Mabel. Please tell me."

"I can't and it's not what you think. Tyler is fine. Turn around and drive safe. We all love you, Gertie."

"Okay. I already turned around and I'm on my way," I cry. "Love you, too."

The line dies. What could have Tyler at the hospital… and Rick? Oh, no. What if it's Tyler mom? Please, God, that family has gone through enough. The warm feeling I had just on the outskirts of Eufaula is gone. I'm scared. If this affects Tyler, it affects me. Oh, no! What if something's wrong with him? Is he dying?

Throwing the car in park, I run toward the emergency room spotting Rick almost instantly. What on earth is he wearing? *Glitter pants?*

"What's going on?" I yell from about twenty-feet away. He looks like hell. His hair's a mess and looks like he's been up for days. "What's wrong?" I repeat.

"Nothing." He wraps a protective arm around me and leads us inside.

"Don't tell me nothing. We're at a fucking hospital, Rick!" Crap, dirty looks surround us.

"Come on, follow me." He removes his arm and proceeds forward. "Ma'am, could you please let me back in." She nods and opens a secured door.

"Where's Tyler? Did something happen?"

"Well, sort of. I'm sorry, Gertie, but I have to take you to him. This isn't my story to tell."

"What?" I ask dumbfounded.

"No, don't worry. He's fine. And don't go thinking that it's Gram either or his mom. It's fine."

"I don't understand."

"Please, just wait and let Tyler explain. And, I didn't tell him you're here. Be easy on him." I stare at Rick wondering what Tyler being at the hospital has to do with explaining anything.

"Follow me," Rick responds sadly as we go around a corner.

I fall in step behind him and wring my hands. Eyes remain on the back of Rick's shoes. I can't bear to look around. My head and heart are in war with one another.

After what feels like endless halls, Rick pushes a button on the wall to enter a closed off unit. My eyes immediately rise to read the name of the unit we're entering: Pediatric Oncology. *What on earth?*

I slip through quickly continuing on my pursuit for answers. Rick waves to the nurses at the main desk and they buzz him through. I stand stunned. *Why are we here? Does he know someone who has cancer? A child?*

My heart sinks while my chest becomes heavy. Vision tunneled, I search for someone who can help me. The woman at the desk smiles and asks if I need to go inside with Rick. Shocked, I find myself nodding.

Walking through the doors, I don't see Rick any longer. As I slowly walk down the corridor, I look into each room worried I might find Tyler—or that I won't. I'm not sure what kind of outcome I want here because it doesn't feel right. No, something's wrong.

When I turn the corner, I hear Tyler's booming voice and giggling. "Aunt Rick, daddy got me a new bear." A little girl shouts excitedly.

Daddy?

Aunt Rick?

I gasp for air, as I'm unable to catch my breath. I wait for my breathing to calm, close my eyes, take a deep breath, and face whatever is on the other side of the wall.

Step.

One small step after another.

Trying to keep in mind what Mabel said, I take another needed breath. A chair holding Gram comes into view. Our eyes lock, and she can tell now is not the time to talk to me. Next, I spot Mrs. Jackson sitting next to Gram chatting away not realizing I'm here. Tyler and Rick's backs are to me. They're standing over what looks like a hospital crib.

I take another step to get closer and find out whom this person is. "Hi!" the little girl with a knitted bonnet says cheerfully. Tyler jumps and spins around. He takes in my large eyes.

"Gert," he whispers.

My eyes fill with tears for a little girl who's lost her hair, clearly from chemo. She's beautiful. And that smile. *Oh, my God!* I know that smile…

It's Tyler's.

I gasp and shoot my eyes to Tyler. "What's going on?" I ask with tears falling freely. He stands like a deer in headlights.

"Gert…" He can't finish.

I shake my head. "Is she… uh… your daughter?" I manage.

He closes his eyes and replies softly, "Yes," as tears begin to spill down his cheeks. My heart stops wanting to soothe his, wanting to take away the pain of his little girl having something wrong, but I can't.

He has a daughter?

He didn't tell me.

Why?

Without a second thought, I turn and leave faster than he can catch me. I know his loyalty is with his little girl so he won't be chasing after me. How could he do this? The man I love with all my heart has a daughter.

Somehow, I make my way back downstairs to the entrance. Shit, do I go to the car? What am I supposed to do? I need to leave. But, look what happened last time I didn't let Tyler explain something. As my mind races, I realize they've all known about his daughter, and I don't even know her name. Oh, my God, I'm such a horrible person. I have no idea what her name is. I left. She's going to think I'm crazy.

Finding a corner outside, I bend over and throw my head in my hands and cry. Life as I know it, or thought I knew it, doesn't exist. How can Tyler keep his daughter from me? Why has he not mentioned her? Please, God, don't let him be ashamed of her. She's so beautiful.

Her complexion, her eyes, her smile... my God, it's *all* him! My fingers lace my hair, grasping chunks so that I can feel pain somewhere other than my heart. Squeezing my eyes shut, I internalize the pain so that I don't look like a complete whack job outside the hospital. I mean, seriously, people are sick beyond those doors and here I'm crying over feelings.

I want to scream *FUCK*, but I don't. I already got visual reprimands for saying it earlier around people. No, I squat quietly grasping my hair and cry in a corner away from reality and those who... I don't know... might know everything.

I'm such a fool.

"Gertie," Rick coaxes, covering my bent form with his. "I'm so sorry you found out like this."

Quickly, I stop crying and stand. My arms reach up pushing him away. "You knew this whole time, didn't you?" I spit.

He looks around at those witnessing my anger. "Gertie, you need to—"

"NO!" I point at him. "He has a daughter and no one told me." I throw my hands by my side after screaming at my friend, who never has since I've known him, lied to me.

Until today. *At least I don't think he has.*

I turn into the brick-walled corner to hide from the world. His hand reaches out. "I'm sorry, Gertie." I shake my head trying to get him to go away. I don't want him here because I need to process this.

Hands that my body instinctively knows soothe my back before pulling me into his body. We wrap our arms around each other and cry. In a very public spot, we grieve together without a care of who witnesses.

"Gert... I didn't want Abigail to be the reason you came back to me," Tyler cries. "I wanted to know that I was enough. If you found out about Abby, you would have been by her side the moment you knew."

I sob loudly knowing he's right. My heart is breaking so hard and I don't know what to do to fix this.

"I love you, Gertie." Tyler rubs my head trying to soothe my pain when it's his daughter that's upstairs who has God knows what.

"Who's her mom?" I ask.

"Cindy," he says pulling away to look me in the eye.

I can't watch from the pain in my heart, so I close mine.

"Gert, Cindy isn't a part of Abby's life," he confesses causing me to spring my eyes open.

"What? Why?" I ask confused all the while hurting for Abby not having her mom to depend upon.

"She... uh..." Tyler closes his eyes and leans his forehead onto mine. "She died during childbirth," he finishes.

I gasp wondering how he's handled this all on his own. No words said—only felt. The one's we want to keep to ourselves. *He's a single parent?*

"How have you been able to visit?" I finally ask.

"Mom's been here helping me with each treatment and trying to figure things out. When dad passed..." He pauses and I cut him off.

I stand up. "Dammit, Tyler! I love you. Stop keeping stuff from me. Stop lying. Stop concealing and just let me in. Do you not know what I mean when I say I love you? I love every part of you." I turn around and shake my head. "I've loved you since we were kids. God, Ty!" I pace some more while he stands still allowing me to process everything. "What's wrong with her?"

"Wilms' tumor."

"What's the prognosis?" I ask praying to God Tyler tells me something positive.

"She was diagnosed two months ago with stage four. It's very rare for children her age to have that advanced of a case and the earliest it's been reported before Abby was the age of four. They removed one of her kidneys and gave her a couple rounds of chemo before we realized it had spread to her lungs. Only a small percent of patients with this disease have stage four. The doctors are optimistic, but it's a hard road." He takes a deep breath. "I'm sorry I didn't tell you, baby." He pulls me into a hug while I try to fathom the enormity of the situation. "I'm serious. I love you and needed to make sure you came back because you want me," he stops... "because..." he takes a deep breath, "there's a possibility Abby won't make it." He begins to cry into the crook of my neck.

Holy shit!

Her mom died?

He's right. I would have swooped in after what I experienced with my parents. I need air.

Dammit!!!!

When the hell is life going to get easy or fair? I don't know how to handle any of this.

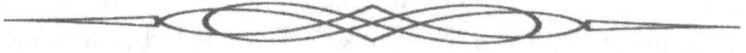

Finally pushing Tyler to return to his daughter, I pull out my phone to call Mabel. She knows. I know it in my heart. That's what she couldn't tell me.

"Hello?" Mabel answers groggily.

"How could you not tell me, Mabel? Why did everyone know, but me?" I cry.

"Gertie, I couldn't. There is no way you would accept her if you didn't see it for yourself." I sniffle and brush the tears away. "You know as well as I do we didn't inherit all of Gram's genes. Thank God! But, seriously, Gert, we don't tell everyone's business like she does." Mabel yawns.

"I know. I just feel like a fool. That everyone knew about this secret and I... I... feel blindsided."

"Please don't. This has been agonizing for Tyler. Please don't let this be the one thing you can't get past. Gert, give it some time."

"I'll try. I love him so much. I don't think I can walk away. Oh, I didn't tell you. I quit my job."

"What?"

"Rachel and Adam are assholes. I'll tell you about it tomorrow. It's too early. Get some sleep."

"Sounds good. It will all work out. I love you."

"Love you, too."

We hang up and I take a moment to scroll through messages Rachel sent blowing up my phone. Ignoring those, I proceed to one left late last night from Matt Edwards. I listen.

"Ms. Sawyer, I just received your email and am confused. I'm not sure if you were possibly intoxicated and sent it on accident. You are invaluable to this company, and I cannot accept your resignation until I speak with you."

Ugh! That damn keyboard. He thought I was drunk?

Even though it's the middle of the night, I call his office phone and leave a message. "Hi, Mr. Edwards. This is Gertrude Sawyer. I apologize for the misspelled words in the email I sent earlier regarding my resignation. Unfortunately, my keyboard is messed up and some of the keys don't work. I apologize as it does appear unprofessional. However, it is true. I must resign immediately due to some improper conduct from a couple employees at Simple Luxury. Regardless of their harassment and wrong behavior, I do not plan to return to Houston. I apologize for the abrupt decision, but something has come up. I've returned to my hometown and must stay. Thank you for everything you have done to help me in my editing career. Take care and again, I'm sorry for failing to give you the two-week notice required.

Bye."

Hanging up, I lean against the brick wall. Everything I've been working toward the last three years is gone. I just threw it all away. Am I making a mistake?

Twenty-Nine

"I wag my tail and pant excitedly. She's here. I'm so happy I could pee myself. Uh-oh, Mr. Prissy Pants won't be happy. I better hide and pretend I've been asleep this whole time."

~ *Cujo*

Tyler

Utterly exhausted, both physically and emotionally, we all decided to stay at Mom's house. Abby, discharged about an hour ago, is finally resting peacefully like the sun. I stand over her toddler bed and take a moment to thank God for doctors. Gertie wraps her arms around my waist from behind. We both stand quietly for a few minutes before I pull her outside grabbing a blanket along the way. I bring Gertie toward me to rest on my shoulder.

"I'm sorry I didn't tell you."

Gertie takes a deep breath, tightening her hold on me.

"Ty, I don't know what to say. I love you no matter what. You're my best friend and I will be here for you."

She pauses. *FUCK!* "I'm still trying to process the fact that you have a child. I hated Cindy for the longest time, and you, too. Nevertheless, I never would want a child to lose their mother as I did. I'm grateful she still has you."

I lean down and kiss the top of her head. "I understand if this is too much for you."

Gertie raises her head slightly pulling back. I'm scared of what she's going to say next.

"I just need time." She lifts a hand, caressing the side of my face. It feels so damn good. "I have loved you forever," oh crap my heart is going to jump out of my chest, "and I always will. It's just… you cheated on me and created this beautiful little girl."

"Gert," I sigh, "that night I remember thinking about you. It's shitty of me to say, but I know in my heart I thought of you… thought it was you when Cindy and me…" Fuck, I can't say it.

Her hand continues to stroke my face.

"What I did was wrong. Believe me when I tell you how much I hated myself for it. When I found out Cindy was pregnant, I thought it was a trap. She knew how much I despised her for what happened that night. Everyone knew I was waiting for your visit. Hell, it's all I could talk about. I didn't speak to Greg for months because I never wanted to take that first shot. Then I realized that it was my fault. I was the one who willingly took her home and crushed our future—regardless of whether I can remember or not." I pause to catch my breath.

Finally, I continue. "I don't understand what happened to Cindy, but I think she realized quickly that I would do the right thing and support her and the baby, but there was nothing left of me to give her. There was no future. I could only see one person and that was you."

"Ty," I place a finger on her lips.

"Wait, I'm not done. Cindy changed." Gert's eyebrows lift in confusion. "She began taking care of herself. She stopped trying to seduce me, and she actually pushed me to find you."

"What?" Gert gasps.

"Yeah, it shocked the hell out of me at first. Then she said something to me. I think she was in her third trimester when her blood pressure was getting out of hand. She told me..." I stop choking on memories.

"What did she say?" Gert cautiously asks.

Keeping our eyes locked, I say, "She told me that if something ever happened to her, I needed to do everything I can to find you. She said she would want you out of everyone else in the world to be a mom for our daughter."

Gert throws her head down onto my chest and weeps. I pull her tighter trying to find the words to help take away her pain. Too much is being thrown at her, and I can't blame her for how she is feeling.

"Sweetheart, I'm not going to ask you to be her mother. I can't do that to you," I confess, but damn if it doesn't gut me. I want that more than anything. Regardless of how I feel or what I want, I won't ask Gert to do it. She needs to want it.

She shakes her head as tears continue to drench my shirt. "I can't, Ty. It's not right. I don't deserve it."

Brushing her hair, I pray to God for the right thing to say. We rock back and forth on the swing with reality weighing heavy on both of our shoulders. I can't tell her she's wrong, even though I know she is. She'll argue and that's not what either of us needs right now. Time will, hopefully, heal both of us.

"Ty, I need to tell you something."

"What is it, babe?"

"Well, I didn't have the opportunity to tell you earlier because we were worried about Abby. I think it's something you might actually be happy about."

I chuckle. "Oh, really?"

Gert sits up with a smile on her face. This has to be good. "I may have quit my job."

An unforgiveable smile grows on me but damn. "Are you serious?" I ask shocked. She nods. "Gert!" My lips land on hers, and we escape in one another on the very swing that's been witness to so many moments like this.

Gert pulls back. "Ty, I may not be able to be Abby's mom, but I love you and because of that, I will love her forever, too."

This woman is going to be the death of me. She keeps surprising me. No more words are needed. My lips find hers again and the stars are the only witness to our love.

Gertie

Tyler's caresses distract my lingering thoughts to let him know I'm not going back to Houston. I'll tell him later. His lips feel too good to break the kiss. My life may not be leading down the path I wanted when I boarded the plane in DC, but anything is possible with Tyler.

He sadly sits up grabbing my hand and the blanket leading us toward Gram's dock. He lays the blanket down, turns and pulls me to his chest, shielding me from the brisk night air. Wrapping the flying wisps of hair behind my ear, he says, "My heart is burning so fucking bright with you here, Gert." I smile just before our mouths collide. Passion erupts. Before we know it, we're laying on the blanket, clothes gone. The slosh of the lake drowns our moans. The blanket wraps us in a secure package filled with so many gifts—the most important one being our love.

Tyler finally pushes inside. Stars, too numerous to count, overtake my senses. "Gert..." Tyler moans. "You are the only one who can fill the other half of my heart," he whispers the last part causing my heart to speed up to the rhythm of our bodies. My hands find his hips as we express our need without words.

The breadth of love fills the air.

Tyler

"Ty?" Gert asks as the soft waves begin to drift us off to sleep wrapped together.

"Yeah?"

"How did Cindy die?" Is it wrong of me to think her question feels weird as I hold her naked body against mine? But, I'd rather answer now and get it out of the way.

"She was diagnosed with pre-eclampsia at some point. I don't remember how far along she was in the pregnancy, but it was two or three months before Abby was born. Right around the time of Cindy's due date, she called to tell me she was in labor." I pause. "I was walking through one of the sites that had so many fucking problems. I stopped what I was doing immediately and began driving to the hospital. But I was in McAlester, which you know is damn near thirty minutes away. I tried so hard, Gert... I rushed to get there, but by that time, Abby was already born and Cindy had passed away." I grip Gert tighter remembering the colossal of grief, love, and fear all too well.

"Abby stayed in the hospital for a couple days. When the nurses handed her over, they gave me a box filled with Cindy's belongings. I still can't believe her parents disowned her. That's a load of bullshit. Even if they had problems, here's an innocent child's life they could be part of." I shake my head in disbelief. To this day, they've never wanted anything to do with Abby. It fucking breaks my heart.

"I'm sorry." Gert's crushing sorrow nearly breaks me. The enormity of how sad she is about what happened to

Cindy, Abby, and me is overwhelming. Gert has a heart of gold. I couldn't ask for a better person to steal my heart. "Do you know why Cindy died?"

"Not really. Well, the doctors told me, but I don't understand it all. Her blood pressure spiked and she was rushed into surgery. I don't know how or why they couldn't save her. She was at a fucking hospital. Isn't that what they are supposed to do, save lives?"

"Please don't let Abby forget Cindy. As much as it hurts to know who her mother is, Abby deserves to know of her mother and the good person she seemed to be." She pauses. "I wonder if she hid, to some degree, behind a façade," she finishes with a yawn.

"I don't know, babe. She just seemed to change overnight." I watch the clouds moving ever so slightly in the moonlit sky and think about Gert's words. Could something have happened to Cindy? I can't imagine. Stroking Gert's back, I thank the heavens she is back in my arms. Perhaps a small thank you to Cindy is in order, too.

Thirty

*"Why are dogs man's best friend? My human can't decide if he's
even a man. I'm supposed to be best friends with that? He says
his butt whispers perfume, when we all know there is no
whispering going on. And if that's perfume, don't ever use it. It
smells like my ass."*

~ *Cujo*

Tyler

Yesterday scared the shit out of me. Not only did Abby
spike a fever and her blood pressure go up, but also, Gertie
finally met the one thing that could have sent her running
again. I want to cry fucking happy tears like the pansy Greg
says I am. With Abby in my arms, I rock her little body
asleep listening as Mom, Gram, and Gert chat away in the
kitchen while working on supper. Abby sleeps so much
now as her body fights this fucking cancer. Rick is busying
himself setting the table. I don't know what I would do
without his help either. Once Gram took me out of her
purgatory, Rick seemed to work his way into the family.
Mom loves him and it's all I can do not to roll my eyes.

He's kind of like a sister, I guess. The thought has me laughing causing my little munchkin to stir. Rubbing Abby's back, I take in her innocent beauty. The other half of my heart.

Feet shuffling draws my attention away.

Gert.

Gert with Cujo sauntering close behind.

Interesting.

I draw my eyes in confusion. Why is she crying? She wipes the tears away and steps toward me. "May I?" Holy shit! She's asking to hold Abby. If I didn't believe in miracles before, I'd gladly clear the air on that topic.

I smile, containing my beaming enthusiasm and nod. She gently tucks her arms under Abby's little body doing her best not to wake her. "Hi, there, sweetie. I've got you," Gert sings. I stand giving up the rocking chair and watch as Abby quickly snuggles into her arms. My heart is finally complete. Leaning over, I give Abby a kiss as she puffs out a sigh falling back to sleep and then kiss the girl of my dreams.

"I love you."

She smiles. "Your mom wanted me to tell you she needs something."

"Okay, I'll be right back." I hesitate, taking in Abby's snuggling form with my Gert. The vision that flashes before my eyes nearly knocks me off my feet. I hate to walk away as this is the first time Gert's held Abby. I want to witness every nanosecond and burn it to memory. Cindy never had the chance to hold her daughter. I'm not sure why God had to take her, but I will make sure Abby knows about her mom. But this… this moment is like the first time I held my helpless baby girl in my arms. Mom *can* wait. I'm not going anywhere.

"Ty?" Gert questions with tears still running down her cheeks, but making sure they don't land on Abby and disturb her.

"My hearts complete," I admit only this time out loud. Gert takes in a quick breath as her eyes fill with brighter tears.

"I love you," she tries to say without crying or talking loudly, and damn, if my heart doesn't skip again. "She's beautiful."

My arms encircle both of my hearts leaning over the rocking chair. I'll stand here all night if my legs let me. "Gert, I don't want you to feel obligated—"

Gert vigorously shakes her head. "No, she's your daughter. I'm here for both of you."

"But this changes everything."

"It doesn't change my love for you. We just need to focus on her health and everything else should fall in place. Right?" She looks up asking for confirmation.

How the fuck did I get so damn lucky?

Oh, my God, she didn't just quit her job. Holy fucking shit! She's staying here.

Last night, during our many conversations, we both agreed she should move in with Gram. Even though I have a house and want her in my bed every night, we think it's best to not jump into things. I pray this separation doesn't last long. We've known each other for damn near all our lives. Why waste another minute? Another day? Mom losing dad makes me want to finish everything with the house yesterday so that I can have her in it today. We'll most likely spend every chance we can together especially since I live next door, just a few acres away.

This is everything I've been dreaming about since Gram began talking to me again. I dreamt about it before but didn't think it was truly possible until Gram got her hand involved. And now, I'm pretty sure that's why my mom needed me in the kitchen. Only she didn't. Truly, Gram pushed her to hold Abby. The old woman knows that once Gert feels what it's like to hold my little heart, she won't ever leave.

I'm going to ask her to marry me one day. It's too soon, but one day I will ask my lifelong best friend to be mine forever. But until then, we'll get to know one another again and try to make it work.

Gert's eyes are locked on Abby's.

"She'll beat this."

Gert nods. "Yes, she will. If she's anything like her daddy, she'll fight and beat it." A shadow moves in my peripheral vision. Gert and I both look up to find Mom, Gram, and Rick watching us with matching tears. I stand pulling Mom into a hug. This has to be so hard for her knowing it's exactly what dad wanted.

"She's home, Ma." Mom's arms tighten at my declaration.

"Yes, son. She's home and it will only be a matter of time before..." I shake my head knowing what she's going to say.

"Let's not jump to conclusions. It's all too new for her."

Mom nods knowingly.

"It's time for supper."

"Okay, let me put Abby down." I walk over to Gert and motion with my arms that I'll take her. Gert shocks the hell out of me by shaking her head no.

"Supper's ready." I make sure she heard.

"Go on and eat, I need a few more minutes." I stand stunned not really knowing what to do with myself. Abby's needs have weighed solely on my shoulders. Although I have a large support system thanks to family and friends, I've always been the one, when around, to take care of Abby. It feels bizarre to allow someone else to take over, but I must admit, a small part of me is chanting something stupid like a cheerleader.

Gertie

Abby's little breaths tickle my chin as she sleeps soundly. It's the cutest thing. The poor thing is so tired. My finger brushes her beautiful face. Thankfully, Ty listened and grabbed a bite to eat. He's worried constantly today.

Taking notes of her temperature, the color of her skin, and what she's eaten, which hasn't been much. Same as Tyler. I might be enjoying this moment too much to let her go. I never allowed myself to think of being a mother. The pain of not having Tyler in my life probably kept me from envisioning the possibility—instead I drowned myself in school and then work.

Now that I don't have a job, I hope Tyler won't mind if I help out while he's at work. We haven't discussed it. I don't want to step on his toes or upset Abby's schedule, so I'll have to wait and play it by ear.

Lullabies I remember Mom singing come to mind. Without even realizing, I start to hum *Twinkle, Twinkle Little Star,* and I get lost. Abby might be the star I needed. The star Tyler needed. She shuffles a little in my arms and I adjust her to a more comfortable position. Life doesn't seem fair for her to go through this.

Leaning my head back, I pray God will kill the cancer and keep Abby here.

I move on to sing another lullaby and then another until I nod off myself.

I jolt at the flash and click. "Gram!" I whisper yell. She rolls her eyes and shushes me with her hand.

"You look like a natural, Gertie." Her pointed stare has my full attention. "I know this must be hard for you, but God works in mysterious ways. I have no doubt in my mind that you will make peace with this and become a large part of that little girl's life."

I shake my head no. "I can't be her mom, Gram. She had one. No one can replace a parent." Cujo sits up and licks my knee. I try to push him away, but the cootie-ridden thing is persistent. Much like his owner.

Thirty-One

"And humans say I do crazy stuff! My human is downright looney bin material."

~ *Cujo*

One week later...

Gertie

"Aunt Rick, come home?" I chuckle every time she refers to him as her aunt.

I nod my head. "Yes, sweetheart. He's on his way."

"Cudo?"

"He's bringing Cujo home, too. Are you excited?"

"Yep," she responds popping her 'p' as she busies herself coloring. We've been drawing pictures for about five minutes. Before that, we danced around to the music. Before that, we watered Gram's flower beds. Before that, we played with her favorite plastic connecting doohickeys. I forget what they're called. Before that, we ate breakfast.

Want to know what time it is? Ten in the morning and I'm ready for a nap! Holy moly, this girl has the energy of a monkey when she feels good.

Even living with Gram, I've had the pleasure of watching Little Miss Busy every day Tyler goes to work. Today, Abby is spending the day with me at Gram's house. Rick went to Houston to pick up a few things for me and should be home this afternoon. I miss Mabel. That's the only downside to moving back home. Living with her afforded me the opportunity to see her anytime I wanted. We've never been apart for long. I don't think I appreciated the time we had together before. Even though we talk every day, it's not the same. I hope she'll be able to visit soon.

I've learned it's important to keep Abby's health a top priority. Not that I'd do anything to jeopardize it. However, we need to keep her home. Taking her out into the public could potentially subject her to viruses that lead to harming her fragile immune system. I don't mind, as I'm not sure I'm ready to face friends who I abruptly left behind years ago. One-step at a time is how I'm approaching all of this.

"Gerbie?" I smile.

"Yes, sweetheart?"

"You color." She hands me another crayon. Lost in thought, I didn't realize I had stopped coloring. I willingly take the blue crayon. Something as simple as coloring makes the world of difference to this little girl.

Coloring doesn't last much longer, and we find ourselves in front of the television watching one of her favorite cartoons. She eagerly snuggles against me, and I find my arm instinctively wrapped around her. There is no way you can't love this little girl. Her head sports a bonnet along with one of her daddy's favorite hats. Tyler would give her the world if he could. He's an amazing father. I never thought I could love him more, but watching him care and play with his munchkin has my heart beating faster. I truly hate myself sometimes for leaving. It may have made me stronger, more accepting and understanding, but it sucks to know what Tyler has had to go through all this time. I want nothing more than to help take some of the emotional burden off his shoulders. Abby is in no way a burden—she's a gift. However, her illness wears on Tyler, and I see where he needs the emotional and physical support. If I can take a little bit of that off his shoulders, I think it will help me move past my regrets.

Maybe.

Cujo jumps on my lap waking me from my little catnap. I try to push him away, but the dog is bound and determined to lick me. *Ack!* I look over and see Abby still curled up in a ball against me, asleep as well.

I glance up and find Rick unloading his arms on the family room floor.

"Gert," he whispers. I raise my eyebrows not wanting to talk in fear I'll wake Abby. She needs her rest.

"You need to get to the cellar."

I mouth 'what' in confusion.

"A wall cloud is headed this way. The radio is blowing up with alerts. Here, I'll grab Abby. You get her blanket, stuffed dog, and medical bag." Rick walks toward us and pulls Abby into his arms, waking her. She protests in return reaching for me. *Oh, my God.* No time to process how much this little act means, I grab Abby and Cujo's leash and head straight for the cellar. The sky is alive with an eerie color of yellow and green. Tree limbs dance in the breeze as a few of Gram's pots over turn leaving them victim to whatever is headed our way. I hate tornadoes. They scare the shit out of me.

I don't ever remember the sky being this haunting. I need to alert Tyler. Abby's head remains tucked under my chin as we run across the lawn. I try to block her from the dirt sandblasting every inch of our bodies.

Rick follows close behind after retrieving Gram from her vegetable garden. We climb down the steps and settle inside. My heart races.

"Wait! What about Tyler?" I ask Rick nervously thinking he had already been warned and on his way here.

"I don't know. I've been trying to call him," Rick tries to assure me.

"He's down by the lake working on the dock," I yell over the wind.

"Okay, I'll go warn him. You guys stay here."

"Daddeee!" Abby cries.

"Rick," I yell again, "please find him and be careful."

"I will, baby girl. Abby, it's okay. I'll go find your daddy, okay?" He gives us each a kiss on the forehead and Cujo a pat on the head before he leaves. Cujo lies against my body while I safely hold a sad Abby. Please, God, don't let there be a tornado. Please, God, keep Tyler and Rick safe.

"Daddeeeee," Abby cries again. I rub her back trying to soothe her fears.

The cellar door opens and Mrs. Jackson disheveled appearance is proof enough the winds have become worse. She closes it behind her. The poor woman's hair is windblown and her clothes are a mess. She looks at me with concerned eyes. Her worry changes to relief finding Abby in my arms.

"Come here, Abby. Nana's here," Mrs. Jackson offers. Abby turns into my chest wanting me to hold her. How can a little girl I just met want me over those who have been here all along? What is it about me that is so comforting to her? I kiss the top of her head as she continues to whimper and cry for Tyler. Mrs. Jackson smiles perceptively.

"I was on my way over to see you when Rick flagged me and said to come out here," Mrs. Jackson says. I nod at the woman whom I love dearly. She will always be my second mom, but right now, I need to focus on keeping Abby safe and distracted. The last thing she needs is to sense any panic. Mom would have done the exact same thing for Mabel and me.

I look down at Abby as her cries have now turned into sad huffs and puffs. Her sweet little fingers fiddle with her favorite blanket. It's gone everywhere with her. It was her small sense of security throughout her hospital stays. I've learned we don't go far without it. Even watering Grams garden earlier, she sat in the chair with her blanket instructing me which flower needed water. It was cute. Damn, those flowers are taking a beating.

I can't wait until she gets stronger. I'm sure water fights will be in our future. Tyler always loved to play. I smile at the memories of us as kids come to mind. He always won, of course. He won at everything we did, but never rubbed it in my face. As we got older, games soon turned into passion and us making out. My God, I love him.

The wind picks up rattling the door. Gram stands to lock it. "Wait! We need to..." I shout over the howling wind.

"Daddeeee."

Gram places a finger on her lip to shush me. "They will go to Tyler's cellar. It will be okay, Gert."

"Gram is right. Tyler and Rick will find their way to safety," Mrs. Jackson reaffirms. I nod as my vision clouds and worry for their safety has me shaking.

"It's okay, Abby. Daddy's safe. Daddy will be okay." I try to make my voice sound assuring only I'm not sure if it's enough to make me feel better.

I just got him back. This can't be happening. Abby begins to fuss more, and I realize she can feel my nervousness. I take a few calming breaths while Cujo licks my leg. I need to be strong for her.

Wow, could Cujo be protecting me? When I first met him, I was stressed and upset finding Tyler and Cindy. Did Cujo snarl at Tyler and not me? All this time, I thought he was ready to sink his teeth into my rear. Maybe... *nah.* That's silly talk. But dogs are protective. Like right now, lying beside me. He's protecting Abby and me. Damn, I just want to pat him on the head and say, 'Good boy,' but then he'll think it's an invitation to express his love and that's just not necessary.

The door rattles harder. "Gram, is there a radio in here?"

"Oh, yes, there is." Gram fumbles through a few items locating the old radio. Crap, it looks as old as she does. She turns it on and the warning sounds 'beep, beep, beep' and mixes with the thunderous sounds outside.

"This is a message from the Emergency Alert System for eastern Oklahoma. A tornado warning remains in effect until three-fifteen P.M. central daylight time. At two-seventeen, trained weather spotters reported a tornado. This tornado was located near Ada moving northeast at thirty miles per hour. If you are in the area of Calvin, Lamar, Scripio, Ulan, Hanna, or Eufaula, seek shelter immediately."

There's a pause before the beeps continue. "A tornado warning remains in effect until three-fifteen P.M. central daylight time. At two-seventeen, trained weather spotters reported a tornado. This tornado was located near Ada moving northeast at thirty miles per hour. If you are in the area of Calvin, Lamar, Scripio, Ulan, Hanna, or Eufaula, seek immediate shelter. This storm is heading directly in your path. Trained weather spotters confirmed a tornado. Hail, three-quarter inches in diameter, dangerous cloud-to-ground lightning, and heavy winds have been reported with this severe thunderstorm. Heavy rainfall may obscure this tornado. If you wait to see or hear it coming, it may be too late to get to a safe place. The safest place you can be during a tornado is in a basement or cellar. Get under a sturdy piece of furniture. If no basement or cellar is available, take shelter on the lowest floor of the building and in an interior room or hallway such as a closet. Use blankets or pillows to cover your body and always stay away from windows. If in mobile homes or vehicles, evacuate them and get inside a substantial shelter. If no shelter is available, lay flat in the nearest ditch or other low laying area and cover your head with your hands."

My arms clench around Abby's little body wanting to keep her safe. I can't let Tyler down.

Tyler.

Please, God, let him be safe. Please keep us all safe.

Abby covers her ears as the change in air pressure is felt throughout the cellar. Oh, my God. It's coming. I rub her back hoping to distract her and sing *Grandma Got Run Over By a Reindeer* against one of her hands covering her ear.

She turns around. "Gram?"

I nod. "Gram got run over by a reindeer," and she smiles. *Ha!* I knew that would work. Mabel and I used to sing that song all the time to Gram knowing it got on her nerves. We thought we were hilarious. Gram, on the other hand, was ready for us to pick out a switch for a good lashing. I smile at Gram, who proceeds to roll her eyes, but joins in to help distract Abby.

We finish singing when the sound of a freight train barreling through goes by. It seems to last forever, but I know it was less than a minute. Hail beats down on the cellar door, and I pray it's just a matter of time before it's over.

I fluff Abby's blanket wrapping it around her tight. Maybe it cocooning her will help her feel safe. Maybe it's helping to distract me from my thoughts of Tyler and Rick. It doesn't take long for the rain to stop. We wait another twenty minutes just to make sure it's safe before opening the heavy cellar door.

Gram and Mrs. Jackson exit first while I put the leash on Cujo. Sitting Abby on the ground, I lift the dog and hand over the leash to Mrs. Jackson. Reaching back, I pull Abby into my arms along with her blanket and bear. Thankfully, Gram grabbed the medical bag, one less thing for me to worry about. My focus is on getting Abby into the house if there is one and then to find Tyler and Rick.

Climbing the ladder, I almost lose my footing. The sun is shining and only one tree uprooted—oh, wait… Gram's poor garden is destroyed, but her beautiful country home still stands. I search to find movements, hoping Tyler and Rick are out of harm's way and looking for us. There isn't any indication they are around. My heart sinks into my stomach. I can't lose him now. *No, no, no, no.* This isn't it.

"Gerbieeee," Abby points to Gram's garden. Oh, I was hoping she wouldn't notice just yet. The poor thing has been through enough with her health. Everything else should be easy and predictable.

"We'll fix it. I promise. That could be something we do together, okay?"

"Uh-huh," Abby sniffs into my neck holding onto me for dear life. Gosh, my heart hurts for her.

Gram puts her arm around my shoulder as we walk into the house. I try so hard not to cry, but it's impossible to contain it. "He's fine. We must put it in God's hands," she whispers for only me to hear. Even though her words are meant to soothe, they don't. Nothing will until I see Tyler.

Mrs. Jackson picks up the phone to call Tyler, but it's dead. With the landline down, Gram pulls out her cell phone and motions for Mrs. Jackson to follow her out onto the front porch. I need to stay here and keep Abby's attention diverted. Pulling the crayons out, we begin coloring again. Cujo sits calmly next to us.

"Abby?"

"Uh-huh?"

"I love you," I try to say hiding my fear for Tyler's safety.

"I wuv you, too."

My leg bounces uncontrollably, and I constantly glance at the screen door hoping Tyler will come through it at any moment.

Gram and Mrs. Jackson walk inside with despondency written all over. *NO!*

"We can't get ahold of either one, Gert." Gram's grim features have me needing to get out there and search. "But I did leave a message for Mabel to let her know we are all okay." Gram winks trying to assure me everyone is good.

"Mrs. Jackson," I calmly address, "will you please color with Abby? I need to go check on something." Abby looks up nervously. "It's okay, sweetie. I'll be right back, okay?"

"K," she answers returning to work on her masterpiece.

"I'll be back," I call out to whoever is listening. I'm through the screen in seconds with Cujo pushing his way through as well. I run to Tyler's house. It doesn't look like a tornado ripped through here so that's got to be a good sign. My feet slosh through the soaking grass. Birds sing as if nothing ever happened. There is only a slight breeze. "Cujo, I need your help. Find Tyler and Aunt Rick." As if he understood everything I said, he charges forward with his nose heavy on the ground. The first place we should check is Tyler's cellar, but I don't know where it is. He took me on a walkthrough of his property, except down by the dock. He says he wants it to be a surprise. I don't remember ever seeing a cellar, although Gram was the one who mentioned it. It's got to be here somewhere.

Cujo's nose works in overdrive turning left and then right before kicking into a sprint. *Oh, my God.* Did he find them? I try to keep up, but the lazy mutt is too fast. Tyler's yard is a mess, but still not enough destruction for a tornado. Cujo begins barking incessantly. I hurry around the side of his house and find Cujo barking at a fallen tree. Please, God, don't let Tyler be crushed underneath it. My eyes wonder looking for shoes, a hat, or even a body part. Nothing. Cujo continues.

I slow down as my heart races forward. Dumb dog doesn't know what the hell he's doing. A scream burns my ears and there is only one person who owns that sound. Rick. I pick up my pace and see what could be a metal door. The tree is resting on top of it.

"Rick… Tyler…" I shout but can't hear anything over Cujo's booming bark. "Cujo!" He stops and I hear Rick and Tyler yelling. Well, Tyler's yelling. Rick, on the other hand, is doing something close to screeching.

I fall to the ground working eagerly to brush away the dirt to find the handle. "Tyler, are you in there?"

"Gert! Are you okay?"

"Yeah, we're all okay."

"Abby?"

"Yes, and your mom and Gram, too. We're all good."

"We can't get the door open."

I laugh while shedding happy tears. "That's because a tree fell on top." I try to roll it over, but the damn thing is too big and heavy. It's probably as old as Gram. "I can't move it, Ty."

"Go in the garage and get the chainsaw."

"What?"

"Gert, focus. You need to cut the tree in pieces so you can manage to move it piece by piece," he yells.

"Oh, okay. Hold on."

I run to the garage while Cujo sits guard. Holy shit, why does Ty have so many tools. I mean, yeah, he's in construction and all, but damn. This is enough to prepare for anything. Thankfully, I know what a chainsaw looks like. I open the cap and check to make sure there's enough gas. Happy with the level, I replace it before running back. Crap, this is heavy.

"Okay, I've got it. Hold on."

"Gert, please be careful."

I laugh. He knows I've never used one of these things, but watched him many times growing up. I pull the string to start, and immediately, wish I had grabbed ear plugs. Slowly lowering the saw on the large trunk, I squint trying to keep the bark from blinding my sight.

After Lord knows how long, Gram shows up and begins pulling the chopped pieces away. The last piece cut, I throw the saw to the ground. The trunk rolls, but my foot slips and it rolls back. *Shit.* My aching arms can't do much more. I try again, this time rolling around to use my back and legs. The metal door is slippery, but it's moving. Gram helps and we finally get it off the door. Tyler pushes it open rushing up the stairs and picks me up. We lose our balance and fall to the ground.

"Oh, my God, babe, I was so worried."

"Me, too. I love you so much, Tyler. I was scared that maybe…" His lips catch mine and I find myself lost in his kiss.

"For heaven's sake, can you two please stop humping for a minute and help me up?" Rick cries giving Gram a chuckle.

Tyler and I laugh as Cujo nuzzles his way between us. "Good boy, Cujo!" I exclaim.

"Well, you know, Cujo and I have had many conversations. I enlightened him on a few things with you, Gert," Gram announces. "That dog loves you whether you want to admit it or not." She clucks before turning around heading back to her house.

"Uh, hello? There are freaking huge spiders in here. Will someone paleeeeze help a poor guy out?"

Tyler and I stand laughing at Rick freaking out. "You know, we could just leave him there," Tyler jokes.

"What?!" Rick shrieks.

"Kidding!" Tyler says before giving him a hand.

As my heart beats happy, I embrace my sassy friend. "I love you, baby girl."

"I love you, too."

Cujo was invaluable in finding the guys. Maybe the tattoo isn't so bad after all.

"Gert, I know this is hard. I'll be waiting in the car," Gram says rubbing my back before turning away.

My fingers graze a large stone as thoughts of a little Gertie running around with her mommy and daddy come to light.

"I miss you so much. It feels as if yesterday I was sitting in Grams family room when she had to sit Mabel and me down to deliver the news you were never coming back." Tears seep from my eyes. "I'm so scared. My life has changed. I'm back with Tyler, but he has this little girl. She's the sweetest thing. You would love her. She lost her mom, too. She won't have the memories like I do of helping you in the kitchen, Mom or helping you build the swing set, Dad. Why is life so unfair?

"His little girl has cancer and although the doctors think the prognosis is good, I'm scared. I'm scared for Tyler and that Abby won't get a chance to enjoy life.

"I want to spend the rest of my life with him, Mom and Dad. Gram said you both used to watch Tyler and I play as kids. Daddy, did you really think back then that Tyler was the one for me? How could you know? I'm scared that I'm not good enough. I'm scared to be a mom. I ran away from Tyler when he needed me most. How can I be a good mom if I did that to him? I can't break that little girl's heart." I fall to my knees and grieve the loss of not only my parents, but for Cindy, too.

"I can't imagine how Gram picked up the pieces to raise me and Mabel when she just lost you, Dad. How can someone be so strong?" Birds chirp above singing their praise for sunshine and maybe that the storm didn't hit here. I'm not sure.

I sit with my back against their combined headstone as I did so many times before I ran. Talking to my parents helps get rid of some of the rawness I still feel. Closing my eyes, I allow the slight breeze to dry my tears. It's soothing, like a blanket covering my fears. It's my parents telling me it will all be okay.

As I stand to leave, an overwhelming sadness takes hold. Mr. Jackson. Eufaula, being the small town it is, has one graveyard. He's here somewhere.

"I love you, Mom and Dad. I'll do my best to make you proud." I kiss their headstone and begin my search for the man who treated me like his own daughter.

So many lives gone. I gasp when I find a familiar name. Cindy. I stare for a moment before sitting down on the cold grass. The large oaks shade this area and I shiver for a second.

"Cindy. I honestly don't know what to say. I hated you. You took advantage of my boyfriend when he was drunk. For the longest time, I despised you for doing that. You knew how much I loved him, but did it anyway." My fingers run along the blades of grass nervously. "But I don't anymore. I'm sorry I hated you and more importantly, I'm sorry for what happened. Your daughter is beautiful. She's a ray of sunshine. Tyler's done an amazing job of raising her. She has this illness, I'm sure you know, and I pray to God that it doesn't take her. I'll never replace you and I don't want to, but I'm going to be here for Tyler, and if that means I take care of Abby too, then I will." I pause as a sob erupts. "I lost my mom and dad and don't ever want your little girl to feel lonely. I had Gram to make sure I was loved and cared for, and I think that is what I'll do for Abby. I love Tyler so much. Thank you for giving him a chance to see the real you before it was too late. That is the person I will tell Abby about because I think you were a good person. It's just... I don't know. Sometimes things happen, and we lose sight of what's real and important. Okay, now I'm rambling. If Mabel was here, she'd already have told me to shut up." I laugh. "When I get a chance, I'll bring Abby by to see you if it's okay with Tyler. Just know that because I love Tyler, I love Abby, too."

Standing, I continue along searching. Along the last row, I almost give up and go to the car to ask Gram for the location. Mr. Jackson's lonely headstone appears. I wrap my arms around it. "I'm so sorry I left without saying goodbye. You were always good to me." I lay my head on top of the marble as if it's his shoulder. "I miss you and so does Tyler. I never wanted him to feel the way I did when I lost Mom and Dad. You know I've come home to stay. I won't leave him again, I promise. I love him so much it sometimes hurts. I've always loved him, Mr. Jackson. I'll take care of him and Abby. I'll do my best to be the person you always made me believe I was. Thank you for being a dad to me. Fixing my bumps and scraps and not telling Gram when you caught Tyler and me making out." I laugh. "Okay, that's a little weird to be saying right now. I just want you to know you mean so much to me, and I will cherish you always." I continue to lay my head on his stone with my hands wrapped around tight not wanting to say goodbye.

I kiss the marble. "I love you, Mr. Jackson." And with that, I stand and walk where Gram is waiting. I walk toward the future God has blessed me with regardless of how different he painted a picture for my future.

Thirty-Two

"I'll be damned if they take his balls, too. Mr. Prissy Pants told me we were going to visit Gertie. I woke up to a cone around my neck and stripped of my manhood."

~ *Cujo*

Six months later...

Gertie

I'm so excited. Today I move in with Tyler and Abby. It marks the beginning of so many possibilities. We've had a few ups and downs with Abby's health, but the doctors now believe she is in remission. We'll have to go in for another scan next month. There are some spots the doctor's question. They don't know if they're tumors or scar tissue. The poor little thing has been through so much but takes it all in stride. She's matured beyond her years with all of the hospital stays and being around adults most of the time. Tyler and I hope to put her in preschool next spring so that she'll be able to be a kid. Her immune system is getting stronger every day and by spring, she should be able to handle anything.

Tyler has me blindfolded saying he has a surprise. I can't wait to see the dock.

"Are you ready?" Tyler whispers in my ear causing a shiver to go up my spine. I'm ready to grab him and make a run for inside!

"Yes, hurry," I answer and he chuckles from behind. Lifting the material hiding my vision, I gasp once it's removed. "Tyler... is that..." My hand covers my mouth in shock.

"Yes, Mom said it belongs here." I yelp turning around to throw my arms around the man I love.

"I can't believe she gave us her porch swing."

"Come on, there's more." He pulls me to the side of the house. *More?*

What has he done?

Roses line both sides of the brick path Tyler had Greg's landscape crew build. The intricate brickwork along with the numerous shrubs and flowers sends me to a faraway land. One that is enchanting and magical. I gawk around trying to take it all in. It is just so much.

I turn to Tyler whose face is beaming. Grabbing my hand, he pulls me further along the path until a dock, much like Grams, comes into view. *Oh, my. It's gorgeous.* I cover my mouth again in surprise with my free hand as tears blur my vision. He told me he had a surprise for me, but wouldn't tell me what it was exactly. I know he's been working on his dock, but this… I never expected something so beautiful.

The brick walkway is perfect for Abby's little feet to walk safely without stumbling. The little things he does for his daughter simply amaze me. Immature trees line each side as well offering shade once they grow and mature.

"Gert," Tyler whispers, "I had the trees planted for Abby. As they grow and spread their branches, so will she." He pauses. "The knockout roses will continuously blossom over the summer months as a sign of my devotion to you. Although they have thorns, their beauty prevails. We are going to hit road bumps along the way Gert, but our love will see through those bumps and we will bloom stronger than before." I gasp as Tyler wipes a tear away. "I love you, Gertrude."

"Oh, Ty." My arms wrap around his neck.

He chuckles. "Come here, there's more."

"More?" I softly question.

He wraps his arm around my shoulder as we proceed down to the dock. I take the opportunity to observe the amazing details he has added—a wrap around railing to protect his little girl from falling into the water and two wooden Adirondack chairs along with a smaller one for his princess. Oh, this is unbelievable. I can't believe the attention to detail he's put into this.

The roar of the motor sounds. Turning around, I find a party boat with OH. MY. GOD. What is Gram and Rick, and… "Mabel!" I screech when she comes into view. Cujo hangs on the side with his tongue nearly in the water. Crazy-ass dog. Oh, and there's Abby.

"Tyler? What is going on?" He stays quiet wearing a huge grin.

"Gerbie, Gerbie, Gerbie," Abby yells. Aw, tiny little fuzz sticks up as her hair follicles heal from treatment and it begins to grow back. It's the cutest thing.

Mabel steps off the boat holding a box. "Gert, I love you and know this is where you belong. You are home. Mom and dad would be so proud of the person you've become. I know you miss them more than anyone does, but here is a clock Dad gave Mom on their thirtieth wedding anniversary. He had a special message engraved." I open the box turning it around to read the inscription. *'The day we met, my heart belonged to you. It will be yours forever.'*

I look up at Mabel who's eyes are filled with love and unshed tears. "Mabel... I love it... thank you." I pause running my fingers along the inscription. "I miss you so much."

Mabel pushes on my shoulder. "Well, you can stop now." I look up questioningly, not understanding what my crazy sister means. "I'm moving home."

"What?" My eyes grow, and I can barely contain my excitement. "How? What about your job?"

"I'll be working from Gram's house. There will be a few times I have to travel back to the office, but I can't see my life anywhere else. This is my home, too."

"Oh, Mabel." I throw my free arm around her and shed happy tears. Tyler pulls the box out of my hand freeing it to join my other. "I can't believe this. This is so exciting." She agrees nodding on my shoulder.

"Okay, next," Mabel announces.

"Next?" I glance at Tyler, who continues to wear a beaming smile.

Rick steps off the boat. "Baby girl, you know I'll do anything for you even though you're boring as hell." I smack his arm. Laughing, he hands me a box.

"What is this?" I ask opening it. A collar and a leash? "What?"

"Gert, I know you and Cujo had a rough start, but he loves you. He helped your stubborn ass see that cooties, especially his, are okay. He protects you and more importantly, he has protected Abby. I cannot see him going to anyone else."

"What do you mean? Why does he need to…"

"I'm going to do some traveling and need someone to watch over my baby."

"Rick… I can't accept this… He's yours."

"After today, he will be where he belongs just like you. I have all the faith that you and Abby will take good care of him."

"Rick," I tackle him in a hug. "You can't go. Please don't leave. I need you."

"Baby girl, you don't need anyone. You are strong and have everything you ever wanted right here. It's not forever. I'm just going to travel a bit, but even if I stayed, Cujo belongs here with you. He's looked after you since the day you eloquently sprawled yourself on the Jackson's lawn." I mix a sob and laugh at the mental image.

"I'd like to forget that moment."

"Oh, baby girl, you met the love of your life that day. He just happens to have four legs. Not only that, but you tattooed him on your ass. He definitely belongs to you." Tyler and Mabel laugh behind me. I look down at the collar and leash in awe. I can't believe this and he's right. I've grown to love the mutt. Cooties and all. Well, until he messes in the house. That will be Tyler's job. Wait, what's going on. I'm so confused.

Tyler walks around taking the box and placing it next to the one Mabel gave me. Rick joins Mabel's side. I look over my shoulder in confusion.

"Mrs. Jackson? What is all this?" She wasn't on the boat.

Smiling, she walks toward me. "Gertie, I love you as if you're my own flesh and blood. I'm so thankful you and Tyler are back together. I will always think of you as a daughter and after today, I would love it if you called me Mom." I gasp pulling her into a warm hug.

"Thank you so much for the swing. I love it."

"It belongs here with you and Tyler. Maybe Abby will create some memories on it just like you two." She pulls back wiggling her eyebrows.

"Ma, let's not go that far." Mrs. Jackson and I chuckle at Tyler.

"Gertie?" I turn around to Gram. "I love you, honey. It might have taken the work of a few," she clears her throat, "to set aside your pride and find your way back home, but you're here. I couldn't be prouder. You are an amazing young lady, granddaughter, daughter, and mother." I gulp. "Don't fight it, sweetie. You are that little girl's mother whether you admit it or not. She needs you and you need her." My arms find their way around Gram. The woman who raised me when I thought my life was over. She lost a son when I lost my parents. But she never made me feel anything but loved. She hid her grief for Mabel and me so that we could feel the security we needed.

"I love you so much, Grammy."

"I have something for you. It's something of your mothers." She hands me a small jewelry box. With shaky hands, I take it. Lifting the top—it's Mom's locket. My hand flies to cover my mouth holding back the sobs. I remember this. She always wore it, holding a picture of Mabel and me. Slowly, I open the locket and find a picture she must have captured of Tyler, Abby, and me—and the other side holds Cujo. I laugh through happy tears.

"Gram, seriously?"

"Of course. That dog played a big part in bringing you home and opening your heart to new possibilities. I mean if you're going to permanently mark your body for him, doesn't he deserve a place here, too?" I roll my eyes at her antics.

"Thank you, Gram. I will cherish it." I smile concentrating on the picture of us. *Family*. We are a family. Why is that so hard for me to grasp?

Abby gently pulls on the edge of my shirt. "Okay, Abby, it's show time," Gram says walking away taking the charm and jewelry box with her placing it next to the other gifts.

Abby's holding an envelope. I kneel down to her height. "Hi, sweetheart."

"I love you, Gerbie." Immediately, I pull her into my arms.

"Aw, honey. I love you, too."

"My mommeee die. Daddeee says she wants you to have dis." She hands me the envelope. I almost don't want to open it for fear I'll read something that will ruin this beautiful moment. Tyler picks up Abby and motions for me to read it. Reluctantly, I do. Unfolding the paper inside, I find a note.

Gertie,

If you're reading this, then something went wrong and I'm no longer here. I have so much I want to say. First of all, I'm sorry. I'm so sorry I seduced Tyler and it caused him to lose you. I know if you're reading this, he's found a way back into your heart. I couldn't be happier for both of you.

I didn't realize what an awful thing it was that I did to you and Tyler until it was too late. I have prayed for God to forgive me and bring the two of you back together. I wished more than anything that I could see my little girl grow up, but God had other plans for me.

I know without a doubt that you will be the perfect mother to my Abigail. I'm sure it hurts to know she's my daughter, but please set that aside and love her with all your might. You and Tyler belong together, and Abby deserves to have a mommy and a daddy.

Please take good care of her like you would a child of your own. You are full of love. Your devotion to Tyler is proof of that. I ask that you be the mom Abby needs.

I will be eternally grateful.

With deepest sincerity,
Cindy

I bring the note to my chest, bend over, and allow the eruption of sobs to flow. Words escape me. For a mother to give their child this opportunity is an incredible selfless act. Cindy is nothing like the person I thought she was. My heart hurts for her. Can I be Abby's mom? Standing tall, I turn to Abby and reach for her. "I love you, sweetheart. I love you so much." I squeeze her tight. Tyler's arms encircle the two of us. Time stops for a moment. "Family," I whisper. Tyler pulls back with tear-stained cheeks smiling.

Cujo nudges me with his nose and licks my leg.

"Come here." He reaches for Abby holding a hand out for the letter. I place it in his hand and wipe my face. I'm a complete mess.

Cujo, annoying as always, nudges and licks me again. Abby giggles, "Daddeee." She places her hand in Tyler's as he walks over to Gram. She takes Abby over to the others.

"Cujo, what is it buddy?" I kneel down to give his head a rub just like he always likes. My fingers hit something unusual. "What's this?" I ask him and nearly fall back on my rear.

Tyler kneels untying a ribbon from Cujo's collar. "Gertrude Ann Sawyer, my heart wasn't complete until you came back into my life. My life will never be fulfilled without you. Gert, I have loved you forever. You are my best friend and will always hold the other half of my heart. We both know life is unpredictable and short. I don't ever want to live another day without you in my life, my home," he pauses and lowers his voice, "my bed." His grin and wiggling eyebrows have me throwing my head back for a second to chuckle. "Gert, I can't imagine life without you. Will you make me the happiest man on earth and marry me?" He opens the box and I am in awe at its beauty.

"Yes," I whisper as Ty removes the ring from the box tossing it aside to take my hand and slip on the sparkling rock. Once he's done, I throw myself at Tyler and he stumbles back taking me with him.

"I love you, Tyler Allen Jackson." I kiss him with all my love. The moment is short lived when Cujo decides he wants in on the action. I squirm to get away causing him to intensify his attempt to get me. Abby giggles from behind and jumps on my back. We wiggle around in a useless attempt to get Cujo away. He's too demanding. Just like Rick.

The three of us laugh along with everyone else. Cujo finally settles down. "Thank you, Tyler."

"For what?"

"For bringing me home."

"Uh, you might want to talk to Gram about that one." He sheepishly looks away.

"GRAM!"

"Oh, dear, look at the time. Church is calling." Gram swiftly walks up the brick path and everyone smiles following her.

"I swear that woman needs help." We both laugh. "I'm not sure I want to know what she did. For someone to write the columns she does, it seems she's missing a bit of tact."

I turn back to Tyler. "Ty?"

"Yeah?"

"This is my family," I admit wrapping my arms around Abby as we lay on Tyler. Cujo gets a second wind and we spend however long keeping away from his cootie-ridden tongue.

"Ahem, I would like to make a toast," Gram stands acknowledging everyone at the table. "To Tyler and Gertie. May you have a lifetime of happiness and beautiful memories."

"To Tyler and Gertie," Mabel, Mrs. Jackson, Rick, and Greg say in unison holding up their glasses. I glance over at

Ty as he winks and sends my hormones into overdrive. I blush and smile over my glass before taking a sip of the cabernet. Greg has been a staple at Grams every Sunday for dinner since the tornado. We are very much a family unit now. Throughout dinner, I kept catching Greg and Mabel's eyes meet. Mabel would quickly look away, but Greg's stare lingered. Could something be going on?

A whine and groan sounds beside me. "Everything okay, buddy?" Cujo puts his paw on my knee. I pat his head and he licks me. For the love of God, this dog loves to use his tongue. It just better not have been somewhere else recently. A quick shiver runs over me at the thought.

The table fills with chatter about Mabel's move and the prospect of Tyler and Greg merging their companies. It's a brilliant idea if you ask me. "I'm going to check on Abby."

I quietly step down the hallway and see my little girl sound asleep with light snores. She's so beautiful. Cujo stands in the doorway taking a break from hogging most of her bed. We had to give him his own blanket after finding him stealing Abby's blanket. He's such a baby.

The thought of having a daughter to depend on me is overwhelming. After I had left Eufaula close to four years ago, I believed my chances at finding love were over. I certainly didn't want to chance another broken heart.

On my way back to join the others, I decide to take a quick detour wanting to find the letter from Cindy and read it one more time. I search Grams antique secretary where the other gifts are placed. My eyes scan and what I find sends my heart pounding. What is this? Why is she writing Gram?

I open the letter and nearly pass out.

Hi, Gram,

I hope this letter finds you well. Simple Luxury is not the same without Gertie and we all miss her terribly. I hope she is happy and everything worked out. Please send me more pictures. She looks so happy. Maybe she'll find a way to forgive me, or should I say, mainly you, and invite Adam and me to the wedding. It is your fault after all. You are a devious old lady and you make me smile.

With love,
Rachel

What the fuck? Gram knows Rachel?

"Darling?" Gram softly questions from behind. I turn shell-shocked and push the letter up so that she knows why I'm upset.

"She… she…"

"I think it's time I plead the fifth." Gram walks back into the dining room with an exaggerated hip sway. Did she plant Rachel? No, that's impossible. An old lady can't possibly be capable of such a thing. Can she? That woman is… is… hell if *I* know.

I shake my head and wonder if any of this truly matters anymore.

I am happy.

I have Tyler.

I have Abby.

I have everything. The rest is just a bump in the road.

Returning to the dining room myself, I smile at Tyler, who leaves his chair to wrap his arms around me.

I am happy.

I finally have it all.

~ THE TAIL-WAGGIN' END ~

Epilogue

"I'm so happy my humans have Gram to look after them. I would have sent them to the shelter a long time ago."

~ *Cujo*

Sunday, March 23, 2014
Drama Queens: Call Off Your Dogs

Citizens of Eufaula, Drama Mama here. As many of us pick up from the tornado that thankfully spared our town, reading is most likely the last thing on our minds. I am so thankful there were no reports of injuries or deaths. That was some storm and definitely left a mess to keep us busy until the cows come home.

I'd like to dedicate this week's column to life. It's such a tricky little bugger. Many are too stupid to see what's sitting right in front of them to enjoy it. We pride ourselves in what we have, but always want more. I don't believe that is the key to a happy life. Nor do I think taking down others lifts your credibility. So why are people so foolish?

Let's take a look at the Indie Author world for a second. Newbies walk around with a cone around their necks as if they were just neutered. Indie Authors would be nowhere if it weren't for the literary giants like Mark Twain, John Steinbeck, Charles Dickerson, and William Shakespeare. These are just a few of the great classic writers.

William Shakespeare wrote in Macbeth, "Fair is foul, and foul is fair. Hover through the fog and filthy air."

Regardless of whether this fits with the dramatics of theatre or not, it makes a statement. How eloquently did Shakespeare write how something might not be as it seems? In the Indie Author world, they appear to work together, but in all actuality, they are selfishly driven. Very few humans are true to their word. Most are hoping to be the next hottest bestseller on bookshelves. I wrote in one of my previous columns comparing dog packs and humans. Dog packs are never competing to get the upper hand. A dog's motives are pure. What you see is what you get. However, in humans, it's much like what Shakespeare wrote—there is a difference in what is and what seems to be.

Life will be full of people like this. It's your job to not be sucked into the façade.

Authors need to ban together. There is a time for one to dominate the other much like my granddaughter and a mutt she thinks she can't stand. The dog is loyal and willingly takes on the submissive role. However, when needed, he will dominate the situation to help her through it. He doesn't dominate maliciously. No, he helps my granddaughter find her way. Much like authors should do for each other.

Earnest Hemmingway wrote, "All modern American literature comes from one book by Mark Twain called Huckleberry Finn... American writing comes from that. There is nothing before. There has been nothing as good since."

If you walk away from the poop obstructing your nostrils, you can learn from the classics. Research your material, dedicate your thoughts to your work in progress, and stop consuming yourself in who's better than the other is. Getting yourself caught up in the 'BS' mentality blurs boundaries. The next thing you know, you're ruining both friendships and relationships with those you work with, and possibly, your future credibility as an Indie Author. For what? To get ahead?

So let me ask you this? When your winning streak ends, and you need the help of fellow authors to grab the attention of your newest book, was it worth the backstabbing, lies, and stories you conjured? Did you really think people wouldn't realize your motives?

If I have any advice to share, and you know I always do, be kind and supportive. Ulterior motives tarnish your reputation and will leave a bad taste in the mouths of your readers. Authors who think they are God's gift because they have blah, blah, blah number of published works that have hit #1 on the bestselling charts aren't better than anyone else. Their poop smells just as bad as mine does. I can't stand to watch authors behave badly. They need a real dose of reality because if it weren't for their predecessors, they'd be nowhere.

Mark Twain also said, "Kindness is the language which the deaf can hear and the blind can see."

Kindness, pups. Neither historical landmarks nor trust can be rebuilt once it's broken. Memories of the trailing storm rushing through your ears cannot be erased just as friendships tarnished. The feeling of the storm will never be forgotten just as words said. A community cannot be rebuilt without having everyone work together. You can duplicate all of these things, but it will never be the same. Suspicion will always be hidden somewhere inside. You will get farther in your career, friendships, and life if everyone bands together.

Society, as a whole, should follow these simple rules. Simple acts of kindness. Whether it's helping a neighbor, a fellow author to find their readers or taking in a stray, if we do our part, what a wonderful world we could share.

So there you have it. Drama Mama's pawprint on life. Stay safe out there, pups. Until next week when everyone has had a chance to recover and put their nods back in place. Thanks for reading Drama Queens: Call Off Your Dogs.

Gram

Ah, I can finally sit back and relax, kiddos. Tyler and Gertie have gotten their heads out of their asses and found their way back to one another with the help of a dog, who I adore, and a dear old Gram.

Life can be so frustrating sometimes. "Isn't that right, Cujo?"

Kindness—now, that's a bone we can all chew on.

Wilms' Tumor

Last year, a friend of my sister's had a nine-year-old grandson, Nathan, who was playing basketball. Suddenly, he began to experience sharp pain in his stomach and blood was found in his urine. First thing you think—urinary tract infection. Right? I think anyone would pray for that diagnosis instead of the one they received.

Nathan's parents called the pediatrician and was told to head straight to the emergency room. The doctors found some things they questioned in his bloodwork. Therefore, they ordered more tests. This is when the mass was found. He was diagnosed with Wilms' Tumor shortly after. As devastating as the news was (is), and after countless hospital visits, treatments, surgeries, he is now, do I dare say in remission? He will continue to be monitored while scans will become a routine to make sure the spots found do not grow in size.

Not many know about Wilms' Tumor. I hope that by providing information here, together, we can raise awareness.

Wilms' tumor is the most common form of kidney cancer found during childhood. It is also called

Nephroblastoma. It's ranked 7% of children's cancer cases with most being diagnosed before the age of five.

The kidneys, like all organs of the body, develop while a baby is still in the womb. Wilms' tumor arises when a mistake occurs in a single embryonic or immature kidney cell. Rather than multiplying normally to become mature kidney cells, this change causes multiplication of new cells that grow out of control, eventually resulting in a mass called Wilms' tumor.

Wilms' tumor is usually found in only one kidney, but sometimes it can occur in both.

Like many masses, a Wilms' tumor may grow until it becomes quite large. Most tumors are discovered before they've had a chance to spread to other parts of the body.

The cause of all Wilms' tumor is unknown. However, some tumors appear to result from changes in one or more gene. In the majority of cases, the genetic changes occur only in the kidney cells and not in other cells of the body. However, in some cases, other parts of the body are also affected.

For more information on Wilms' tumor click here.

Information courtesy of Cure Search.

Playlist

Anyone who knows me knows how much I love music. It can be calming, express feelings, and allow you to escape in movements. I had a large playlist I listened to while writing Drama Queens: Call Off Your Dogs. The list below is of some of the songs on my playlist I wanted to share with you. A few have spotlights in the story. I hope you enjoy.

~ *L.U. Ann*

Don't Speak (American Idol Performance) – *Alex Preston*

* Ugly Heart – *G.R.L* *

Break Up In A Small Town – *Sam Hunt*

** I'm A Mess – *Ed Sheeran* **

My Fault – *Imagine Dragons*

Superheroes – *The Script*

A Sky Full Of Stars – *Coldplay*

Country Girl (Shake It For Me) – *Luke Bryan*

Boys 'Round Here – *Blake Shelton*

Bang, Bang – *Jessie J, Ariana Grande, Nicki Minaj*

She Bangs – *Ricky Martin*

Bailiando – *Enrique Iglesias, Sean Paul, Descemer Bueno, Gente De Zona*

L.U. ANN

I Will Be There – *Odessa*

XO - *Beyonce*

*Gertie's song

**Tyler's song

A Note from the Author

Thank you for reading Drama Queens: Call Off Your Dogs. I hope you enjoyed it. The best gift you can give an author is leave a review on Goodreads and the site where you purchased.

I would be very grateful to hear your thoughts.

Happy Reading,

L.U. Ann

About the Author

Author L.U. Ann moved to Colorado from the Eastern Shore of Maryland with her husband and two children. Life in Colorado is so much different. In Maryland, you would find her in the garden tending to her vegetables and flowers, sea glass and shark tooth hunting once a week, and enjoying the kids swimming in the backyard. Our lives took a drastic change moving to 'Our Little House on the Prairie' at an elevation of over 6,000 feet and the semi-arid climate making it hard to grow anything. While barely anything can grow where she resides now, the wildlife makes up for it. Mountain Lions and coyotes and rattlesnakes. Oh, my!

She tries to spend a little time each day writing, but domestic chores around the house usually take precedence. She would much rather hide the mess from her husband. She tends to her loving four-legged friends, who at times become much too demanding when she locks herself in the office. This often results in MORE domestic work—cleaning up after their deviant behavior.

At night, you'll find her begging the kids to go to bed so she can catch up on the latest book before her sister can.

Yes, she is an avid reader, who escapes her chaotic, but wonderful home to the feisty depths of romance land in search of her newest book boyfriend. Shh, don't tell her husband!

She is an artist by the grace of God. She worked as a set designer for six years, helping establish a local children's theatre where she was the scenery artist, set, and prop designer. Before that, you would find her covered in paint so engrossed in painting a mural that time didn't exist. Graphic design is her guilty pleasure.

OTHER WORKS BY L.U. ANN

A Destructive Novel Series:
Destructive Silence
Destructive Choices
Destructive Release

CONNECT WITH ME:

Email: author.l.u.ann@gmail.com

Website: http://authorluann.com

Twitter: @authorluann

Facebook: www.facebook.com/luann.author

www.ingramcontent.com/pod-product-compliance
Lightning Source LLC
Chambersburg PA
CBHW071241170626
46809CB00001B/45